The Perfect Meal

James D. Kirk

ISBN: 0615518001
ISBN-13: 978-0615518008 (Boldly Going Enterprises)

DEDICATION

With all my gratitude and love,
I dedicate this book to my mother,
Linda Lee.

CONTENTS

1	Fathers Meet	1
2	Chef Didier	8
3	Growing Up	17
4	Birth and Death	21
5	Culinary Dreams	28
6	Admissions Letter	34
7	Unknown Consequences	40
8	Destruction of a Dream	45
9	Reality Sets In	49
10	Enter Angela	53
11	Pen Pals	58
12	Temperature Rising	62
13	Re-Gifting	68
14	Pursuit of the Perfect Meal	73
15	Review is In	78
16	Work, Work, Work	81
17	Friends Again For the First Time	88
18	The Days Before the Last Supper	92
19	Last Supper	98
20	Orphaned In an Instant	104
21	To the Bone	112
22	Fall and Rise	116
23	Angela's Realization	121
24	The Perfect Meal	128
	Epilogue	133
	About the Author	134

1 FATHERS MEET

There was no time to drag his wife and 5 year old son through the harsh New York winter of December, 1976. Gerald was late, and if the research he had done on this new restaurant location proved accurate, he wanted to impress the real estate agent by getting there early. He would be taking a taxi cab this trip and going alone.

"Are you sure you don't want us to come, Gerry?" His wife Betty was attempting to don a coat and hat on her son, Gregory.

"You're beautiful, Bet, but this is a very important first meeting and if we are going to get a good deal on this space, I need to be able to focus. I'll call you when it's over."

Betty's smile dimmed. She waited for a parting embrace but was only graced with a kiss on the cheek as he flew out the front door of their upper West Side flat, briefcase, gloves and overcoat in hand.

"Come back here, Gregory Anderson! Let Momma take off your coat and hat. GREGORY!"

Before Betty could corral him, Greg had ran out the front door, and latched himself to one of Gerald's trouser legs.

"Let go, son. You need to go back inside with you mother. BETTY"

"I want to go with you, Father. I don't wanna stay home with Mother. I want to be with you, please."

Greg was clinging tightly to his father's leg. Betty was unable to break him free.

"Gregory I do not have time for this. Let go!"

But he would not let go. Still holding on with all his might, Greg tilted his head back away from Gerald's trousers revealing wet marks on the fabric, a combination of tears and snot.

Gerald, enraged, dropped everything and violently grabbed Greg's arm. He pulled the small boy off his leg with one hand and slapped the child's tiny cheek with his other. Greg was stunned. His mother, shocked.

"Gerald! That wasn't necessary. I would have taken care of this."

"I'm going to be late now, Betty. Thank you. Thank you both."

------ oOo ------

Raymond and Ruth Walker lived in the Bronx, almost exactly mid-way between the Pelham Parkway and Morris Park subway stations. This made it convenient when they wanted to get into Manhattan. If they needed to head over to the East Side, it was Pelham. West Side, Morris Park.

"Bundle up everyone. It is C-O-L-D, cold, cold, cold out there!" Raymond Walker was part cheerleader, part motivator and all father to little Jeffrey and his oldest, Ray, Jr. Ruth and Raymond had been married since 1965, nearly 11 wonderful years. She'd never known him to be anything less than a best friend and shining example of fatherhood. Watching from a seat near the front door, she attempts to get the gang going.

"Jeffrey, I don't think your father wants to play the one armed bandit right now! Ray, Jr., help your father please?"

Jeff was being aided with his winter wear by a patient, smiling patriarch who on more than one occasion had been unable to find his son's second arm when putting on a coat or sweater.

"Daddy, I only have one arm. I only have one arm, Daddy! Daddy, where's my other arm?! Oh, no, Daddy. I'm going to be the One Armed Bandit!"

At five years older than his little brother, Ray, Jr. had very little patience. "Come on, Jeffy. Cut it out, silly."

"Ruth, brace yourself, my love. One of your sons has lost his arm. You might as well start cutting off those extra sleeves on all his coats and shirts right now."

Playing along, she stood up from her resting place, grabbed some scissors from a nearby desk and started moving towards the loose, flapping sleeve that was hanging on Jeff's right side.

She was making snipping motions with the scissors and the young boy allowed her to get right to the seams on his coat before he reacted.

"No Mommy!" he shouted, forcing his right hand through the sleeve.

"My goodness, Ruth, would you look at that? It's a miracle. It is a miracle I tell you. Our boy has suddenly regrown his arm."

"No, Daddy. I was just playing. I didn't grow another one. If I did I would have 3 arms. Then Mommy would have to make more sleeves for all my shirts!"

Even at ten, the elder son knew what a ham his brother could be. Looking at his parents with Jeff, he could only sigh.

"We really should be heading for the station now, Ray. We don't want to keep the Realtor waiting."

"No, we most certainly do not. Jeff, if we are a little tardy, you lose that arm again and we can say that we are late because we had to spend extra time searching for a lost limb! Got it?"

"Got it, Daddy!"

Jeff was a smart kid, his 5th birthday coming up in January. He took his pop seriously for a few moments before the smiles on his parents faces told him they were only pulling his leg. Ray, Jr. really wanted to pull his leg. Off.

------ oOo ------

Gerald noticed no one waiting in front of the closed restaurant space as the taxi pulled up. "Great," he thinks to himself. This allows him to be the one waiting.

"Keep the change," he tells the driver as he grabs his brief case and exits the vehicle. It is about five minutes before 2 P.M. Five minutes to go over everything in his head he needs to share. He thinks out loud, in a low voice.

"We have at least six months of operating capital in our savings reserve. I've worked on the financial side of the restaurant business for eight years now as well as having grown up in a neighborhood deli. A promising young chef is looking for a minority interest and hopes to make the most of this opportunity with us as well."

Pacing back and forth along the sidewalk, he reviews his facts. He turns and notices in the window's reflection a tired looking restaurant space almost directly across the street. At that moment, Jonathon, his Realtor arrives.

"Mr. Anderson? So good to meet you, sir!" They shake hands and as they exchange pleasantries, Gerald asks him about the space across the street.

"Ah, yes. You can never have too many places to eat, right? If you're interested we can take you over after we show you this space."

"That might be a good way to compare what I'm looking at investing in. Thanks."

The Realtor unlocks the front doors and they enter the waiting area of the restaurant. The owner was wise in that he had everything professionally cleaned.

"This is quite nice," Gerald admitted. "I can appreciate an owner who understands the impact of making the place spot on."

As they move into the dining area, the front doors burst open with four heavily bundled city goers ushering themselves in along with extremely cold, damp air.

Startled, Gerald and Jonathon turn to find the Walkers rosy cheeked and cheery after their travels from the train station to the empty restaurant.

Extending his hand as he walked towards Gerald he exclaims quickly, "You must be Jonathon. My apologies for our tardiness. It seems we had to spend time along the way searching for our son's lost arm. Fortunately we found it and here we are to look at the restaurant. I'm Raymond, but my friends all call me Ray. This lovely creature is my wife, Ruth. The half-pint with two arms is our son, Jeffrey. Beside him is Ray, Jr., of course."

Realizing that the Walkers were interested in the same space he turns to the Realtor completely shunning Raymond's greeting.

"I'm so sorry, Mr. Walker, Mr. Anderson. There must have been a scheduling mix up. Normally, I never have two clients reviewing a space at the same time. Please, please accept my apologies."

Sensing Anderson was going to be less than friendly, Raymond instead offered his hand to Jonathon, repeated his introduction, this time leaving out the tale of Jeff's missing appendage.

"Well it's perfectly all right with us if Mr. Anderson is here. We don't mind at all. Work for you, Mr. Anderson?"

"Fine," he says and turns to go about inspecting the space.

As the Realtor tours the group through the bar, dining area and eventually into the kitchens he performs his qualifying.

"Mr. and Mrs. Walker, do you think this space is going to be everything you are looking for? It is quite large and has most of the appliances already in place."

He wonders if they are just a bit out of their league financially.

"Well, it is lovely, if not a bit larger than we had imagined," Ruth shared. One could tell by the unspoken communications between she and Ray that this was definitely a space they would love. Affording to purchase and get operating would be another story.

Gerald speaks up as if to quash any further dream building on the part of his new competitor. "Jonathon, I think we may have a deal here. Everything is exactly as you've described it to me in our previous conversations. My wife and I have more than enough to close escrow and we would like very much to put an offer in today."

Raymond is irritated by this fellow and feels an ego pinch at hearing the proposal. He knows intellectually they really cannot afford the purchase price, however emotionally he doesn't appreciate Anderson's approach.

"I think we may be able to put an offer in as well. With so much already here we'll have to revise some of our previous calculations, but we should have a written offer for you today. Oh, didn't you mention to me there was another space nearby that you would show us as well?"

"Of course, Mr. Walker. Directly across the street is the second restaurant. If you and your lovely family would like to head over that way, I'll just lock up here and join you in a few moments."

After the doors closed behind the Walkers, Gerald immediately indicates to the Realtor that he has no need to see a space that is inferior to this one.

"Shall I send you over a written offer today? I believe we can make arrangements that are acceptable to the owner and get things moving. Time is of the essence."

"That's most excellent, sir. If the Walkers are also going to submit, I'll make sure to deliver both offers before heading home for the evening."

In Gerald's mind there is no way those people were going to get his space. Opening a restaurant in Manhattan had been a dream of his since he had finally come to accept the family trade. His father and grandfather, given their faults, had beat every other career possibility out of Gerald during his formative years. Now, having found a good space there was no way the Walkers would alter his plans.

Including the several floors of living spaces above the restaurant, he knows this will become the new home and business for his family. He excuses himself as they exit and hails a cab. He will write up his offered purchase price and stipulations, and have it waiting on Jonathon's desk when he returns to his office.

Apologizing for their wait, Jonathon quickly opens the doors of the second eatery, allowing the Walkers to escape the cold. While nice, there was still some left over remnants from the previous business. Clearly the owner of this property did not feel the need to make the same first impression as their last experience.

"Well, I'll definitely be doing some cleaning and organizing here," Ruth said quietly to Jeff and little Ray.

"I can help you, Mommy Just like I do at home."

"Not me. Do I have to help clean this junk, Mother? Can't I just go play in the park instead?" Ray, Jr. clearly had places to go and young people to see.

"There will be plenty of play time for both of you hooligans," Ruth chuckled.

Still a bit ego bruised from his experience with Gerald, Raymond inquires about the living space in this building.

"Yes, there are 2 upper flats that can be used as a single residence, or if you're ambitious you might consider splitting one or both of the units and get several apartments out of the deal. You would have to do some extra plumbing work, but that would pay for itself in no time at all."

Perhaps not as business minded as Gerald, but with all the energy and imagination required, Raymond realized this space would work for them if they were unable to secure their more desirable choice. He pulls Ruth aside as they head upstairs.

"What do you think, Ruthie? You like? I'm sure we can beat out Anderson for that other space but if not, this isn't the end of our dream, right?"

"Honey, don't get riled up about that man. Clearly his head is in a different place than yours. Than ours. Yes, I would love to have that place too, but not if it means we'll be in less of a position to succeed. We are putting everything we own into this. Everything!"

"I know, sweetie, I know. But I still want to try for over there. We'll submit an offer here as well. Okay?"

Ruth is reluctant to agree. She knows her husband's personality. He is a wonderful, loving father and has always been the very best friend to her, but she also knows about his competitive side. His friend's wives tattle about his golf outings with their husbands and Ray not quite playing up to par. She wants the best for her family. She thinks to herself that having the larger, nicer space would be a great jump on making their dreams come true. In her heart she also realizes they just do not have the resources to over extend and win that place.

"Okay, Ray. Okay."

------ oOo ------

Young Gregory was inconsolable. Betty tried shushing, bribing with ice cream, even daring to raise her voice at the boy. Nothing worked. Her husband had a quick temper when it came to the antics of the child. As far as she knew, this slapping was a first. There were still bright red marks the size and shape of Gerald's fingers on Greg's flesh.

"Greg, honey. Mother is going to put some ice in a cloth and hold it on your face. This will make it feel much better, sweetheart." She also hoped it might prevent nasty bruises from forming. Injuries like that required explanations.

After several minutes, Greg sobs to her, "It's very cold, Mother. Now I am cold. Was I really bad, Mother? Why did Father do that? I did not mean to make Father mad."

Greg was on Betty's lap as the two sat in the kitchen. His sobbing continued, though diminished in degree.

"Your father had some very important business on his mind, honey. He has been very focused on his work for some time now. He even gets upset with me, Gregory, so don't you worry. Everything will be just fine."

Removing the towel of ice, Betty checked the injured area. Finger marks could no longer be seen due to the entire cheek having a bright pink hue thanks to the cold.

"Oh, my dear," she cooed, touching his cheek with the back of her hand. "Let's warm that cheek up a bit."

Opening her blouse a few buttons, Betty placed the rosy cheek on one of her slightly more than ample breasts. Even through the brassiere, Greg was subjected to her warm, nurturing, touch.

THE PERFECT MEAL

Finally something seemed to be calming the boy's emotions. The longer she held him next to her, the more relaxed they became. She thought Greg might have slipped off to sleep. When she gazed down, she saw his eyes open. They had a trance-like quality. Periodically the boy burrowed deeper. At one point, quite unconsciously, Greg instinctively reached for and was able to release one of his mother's breasts. He suckled her nipple as if he might have reverted to an infantile mental state.

Several years had passed since she had breast fed and Betty was surprised at the boy's actions. She attempted to dislodge his mouth. His suction was much stronger than it had been as a baby.

Deciding no harm would come, this one time, she relaxed and held her boy close. In short time the rhythmic suckling and tiny hands groping and probing had lulled Betty into a trance as well. The feelings going through her body and mind were something other than maternal.

There had been less intimate activity between she and Gerald since the baby was born, and the sex they experienced had been accompanied by little foreplay. Romance was not even in the equation.

These thoughts swirled in Betty's mind while Greg continued. The longer she allowed him to remain, the more sensuous and feminine she felt. For a brief moment she pondered whether this was wrong. Looking down on his closed eyes, she decided it could not be a mistake.

"Just a few more moments, little one," she whispered.

A stirring inside her flipped a switch, turning something on. Picking up the child, she carried him to bed, laying down beside him. Greg awoke just enough to reach for his mother's breast again and continued to receive her. Betty lay there experiencing a wide range of physical and emotional pleasures.

2 CHEF DIDIER

8:15 pm, June 18th, 1940. Four days since the Germans entered the city of Paris, and already the official French government considered signing an armistice in an attempt to appease that tyrant, Hitler. The people huddled quietly in their residences at night, keeping all dark, praying not to attract the attention of roving enemy soldiers. Patrols even wound their way through every floor in the hotels and apartment buildings looking for radicals and dissidents.

Illumination in the room was due to a single candle and what few lights were still on in Paris after 8 p.m. The bedside radio with its volume low, barely audible to the two present.

"Whatever happens, the flame of the French Resistance must not be extinguished and will not be extinguished. Tomorrow, as today, I will speak on the radio from London."

"Turn him off, Alayna. de Gaulle may have one fewer listening if he is to speak again tomorrow."

Laying on the tiny bed covered neck to toe in heavy blankets, he requested his caretaker to help him sit up.

"I want to gaze upon the enchantress that is hopefully still Paris."

The Free French was whom Charles de Gaulle directed his radio speech. The old man in the bed considered himself of liberal mind, unfortunately his 65 years, mostly of hard labor in the best kitchens in France, had finally betrayed his body.

Alayna has been this man's little rock for 2 1/2 decades, but never more so than now. An unmarried cousin, she was always thankful for his watchful eye, protection, and all he provided her. In return, she kept his home and offered him the creature comforts he needed after long, grueling days in the kitchens.

THE PERFECT MEAL

Didier Ives Devereux had cooked for over 50 years. It was literally all he knew. He knew it well, very well. Chefs traveled the world round in order to work for and learn from this great culinary master just as he had done when his parents deposited him in Auguste Escoffier's kitchen on New Years Day, 1888. This was to be his 13th birthday present. He never saw his mother and father again.

"Alayna," he feebly requested, "would you be so kind as to reach my jacket? I'd like my temperature gauge, if you will."

"I will do no such thing, Didier. You are not getting out of that bed to do any cooking or anything else for that matter."

"Please, Alayna. Do not fight me on this. Kindly hand it to me, my dear woman."

Acquiescing, she was curious of his request.

"Why would you desire such a tool now, Didier? Surely you are not planning to work a meal? You are in no state to move from that bed. I forbid it!" She found the volume of her voice rising, quieted herself and listened for evidence of German soldiers.

His chuckle ended in violent coughing. Alayna offered him some water to sooth his parched throat, but admonished his loud outburst. "Didier, you must try and remain quiet. You know they are near, just waiting to arrest anyone they please."

"Yes, my dear. I shall do my best," his voice barely above a whisper. "And no, Alayna, I fear there is no cooking left within my hands, nor my soul. But as you have been such a faithful friend to have looked after this lonely old man all these years, I wish to share with you the one story I've kept to myself. The story of my true love."

"You must rest now. There will be time for this tomorrow. I shall prepare your favorite teas and toast when you arise."

"Again I tell you no, dear Alayna. This I need to share. Tonight."

"If you insist, my attention is completely yours, cousin."

Alayna wrung out the cloth and lovingly draped it around his neck. The single candle in the room flickered a bit, its reflection twinkling in Didier's eyes. For the first time Alayna notices something on the face of the temperature gauge that reflected the candle's flame.

Seeing her notice the precious gem, Didier attempts to begin his story but more coughing prevents him from speaking. Grabbing a large bowl from the night stand, Alayna helps the old man clear his mouth and throat.

"Shhh. Take some more water, Didier. You really should rest now. Can this story of yours not wait one more day?"

"I am better now, thank you. I shall begin."

We were all quite harried in the kitchen from very early in the morning of a great feast our restaurant had been hired to cook. I'd recently had my

23rd birthday and was in charge of several men creating sauces, soups and the like. Our patron was a very powerful and wealthy businessman, Messier de Bourg. His eldest daughter was to wed that afternoon. We had slaved for many days in preparation.

As with most tasks in cooking, timing is everything. Proper heating temperatures, how long food is on the flame, how long it should rest, even when seasonings need to be administered are all crucial factors in the success or failure of ones cooking. Needing some particular spices, I left the kitchen to search through the pantry. Focused on my task I failed to immediately notice the petite, young woman sitting upon a barrel in the room's corner. As I searched about the shelves I heard her cough, ever so politely.

"Pardon me, chef. My presence here is surely of no inconvenience to your preparations I trust?"

She had been crying and was still visibly emotional.

"Are you all right, my dear? Is there anything I can do for you? Someone I might fetch to aid you during your distress?"

She looked up at me. The light from the kitchen shone through the partially opened door to illuminate her face and hair. It was then I realized what a beauty this girl of maybe 18 years truly was. Again I asked of her well being.

"Please, there must be some way I can help you now miss. Would you care for me to escort you to the balconies where you might get some fresh air and sunshine on this glorious day?"

This prompted her to shed more tears.

"Today my eldest sister is to be married. She is so lovely and kind. I wish her a long, happy life with her husband to be."

I was confused.

"If it is such a wondrous occasion, why then do you hide in this closet, sulking and sobbing the day away? Surely there must be much your sister and others are depending upon you to do?"

"I am saddened at the fact that now I'm the last of my sisters unmarried. My greatest fears are that something will happen to take my parents from me, leaving me alone and at the mercy of the world. I've yet to find true love and if I don't soon, my father will surely arrange a marriage of convenience as he's done with both of my older sisters."

Hearing of her emotional plight I was under her spell. I'd never been in love before. There was never enough time apart from my training in Auguste's kitchens.

"Surely at your tender young age there is plenty of time, no? Here, take my hand and allow me to escort you out into the warmth of the sun which dims in comparison to your radiant beauty."

Moments before she had been in a demonstrative, emotional state. Now she was a coy young woman confronted with a well intentioned kitchen apprentice.

"My name is Didier Devereux, my dear. To whom have I the luxury of escorting?"

"Yasmina Margaux de Bourg," was all she replied. It was the sound of her voice which left the sweetest ringing in my ears.

I helped her from the barrel and walked her slowly to the hotel balconies overlooking Paris. She was visibly tired from her emotional outbreak and yet it seemed there was a new, vibrant aura about her.

"Will you be fine now, Yasmina Margaux de Bourg? Shall I send someone to be with you?"

"You are ever so kind, Chef Devereux. But no. Thank you. Your generosity of spirit has helped guide me to this lovely perch. I will recompose and then seek to perform my duties with the love and devotion any sister should. Again, thank you for your kindness."

"Ah, but the pleasure is all mine. It is I who shall thank you for shining your beauty and emotions on this lowly cook. And I am still a few years from becoming a chef. The great Escoffier tells me I am making progress and shall soon have his blessings to go off and work my own kitchens."

"Well, today you are certainly my Chef. I trust we shall see each other again soon, Chef Didier?"

"Nothing in this world would make me happier Mademoiselle de Bourg."

The chef suddenly had a fit of coughing which Alayna helped with by holding a cool, wet cloth upon his mouth. Looking into his eyes she recognized love and yet, sadness as well.

There were sounds of doors slamming closed on the floor below their apartment. Alayna held the cloth just a little longer over the old man's mouth hoping that he would not get the attention of the unwanted visitors. After a few moments passed with nothing transpiring, Alayna asked Didier, "Did you see her again, cousin?"

"Oh, my. Yes." Less sadness in his eyes now, more love.

The great feast was wonderful. Truly one of our master chef's most amazing meals. Given that I held rank in the brigade, once the final courses went out, the dish washers and line cooks took over cleaning and repairing the kitchens.

I left work and strolled out to the very benches where I'd left young Yasmina just that morning. To my surprise, she was there, once again, at the very bench from earlier.

Calling out to her, "Yasmina? Is that you? All is well in your world?"

As her head turned, the moon caught all of her beauty in its pale light. I may have been dreaming at that point, but it seemed her face and hair amplified those lunar rays.

"Yes, Didier. It is I who have returned to this spot praying you too might find your way back to me."

With that, she reached out for my hand, and I hers, pulling her close to me. She softly held me at bay for a moment.

"In my darkest hour of self indulgence, you helped me understand and find the strength and courage to be the person I needed most to be today. You shared selflessly and I am forever in your debt."

With that she permitted me to cup her lovely face in my hands and kiss her as I'd never done before. Apparently, she had never been held in such an embrace either, as evidenced by the tear tracking down her cheek.

As he related those events to Alayna, she noticed he had been gently caressing the thermometer she had given him earlier.

"But where does the temperature gauge come into the story, Didier? Surely you're not expecting me to use it on you?"

Again he laughs softly with his caring cousin. This time he has more energy and continues with his story.

"Certainly I am at temperature already," he smiled. "It was a gift from Yasmina. Her powerful father had taken a residence at the hotel my mentor, Escoffier, had opened and partnered with Cesar Ritz. It was one of the finest luxury hotels and restaurants in all of France. Having offices and a residence there, the de Bourg's spent much time in the city.

The Paris Ritz had become the place to be at the turn of the century for the powerful and wealthy. Over the next few years we stole moments when no one was looking. On the rare and wonderful occasion we were able to sneak off into the night, we would spend a few hours enjoying food from other kitchens. In her company those were some of the most perfect meals I had ever the pleasure of consuming.

Sadness expanded across Didier's face as he continued.

It must have been around 1903 or so when Yasmina informed me her father was sailing her across the Atlantic. I seem to recall that the Wright Brothers had just made all the papers with their flight at Kitty Hawk.

"Please forgive me, Didier, but I must follow my father's commands and go to Chicago. He wants me to be his eyes and ears as he looks at the possibility of investing in a company that manufactures industrial scales and tools for scientific measurement and such. I'll be staying with the family of one of my father's cousins in Chicago. Apparently this man hopes to entice the Hanssen Scale Company to build and operate a manufacturing plant somewhere in Europe. I'm told the investment opportunity is a rare one and if worthy, my father is to be a major stakeholder."

THE PERFECT MEAL

"But how long will we be apart, dear Yasmina?"

"It may be as long as a year, my love. Please understand. There is very little choice I have in the matter. Being unmarried, my father still has nearly complete control in all I do."

I knew we could not elope and start our lives together. I was still an assistant chef, and one with little standing as compared to the great Escoffier. Yasmina and I both knew her father would not even consider such a union. I had nothing to offer him for her hand in marriage. Love would never be enough for this man.

At first I was distraught about her leaving. The time we had spent together since we'd first met made life worth living. Just thinking upon the future we could have helped me focus on my craft in the kitchen. Her love had opened the cupboard holding both my heart and my passions. Food, love, it all had begun to intertwine. My passion for creating the perfect meal in honor of my dear sweet Yasmina was what tended to get me through most of the days in her absence.

Her letters had a way of lifting my spirits and shining her love's light about my soul. She shared most of what was happening in her life there in Chicago.

"Today, dear Didier, I was taken to a wonderful university in the Urbana-Champaign area a few hours south of Chicago. It seemed the scale company my father is interested in provides tools for various science departments at the colleges here.

"While we were visiting the various laboratories and facilities I came to be introduced to a rather exciting and interesting woman by the name of Isabel Bevier. Apparently, she is one of this country's leading female educators and had just a few years ago taken over the head of the university's Domestic Sciences department.

"Didier, she and I made such a lovely connection that I've decided to accept her offer and attend the upcoming summer course she teaches. My father is all for it as he feels my home economics skills are somewhat lacking. It will add some time to my stay here, but I assure you of my return in mid-August."

So, I was to wait several more months for my true love to return. I had no choice but to continue loving Yasmina from afar.

The Russian Revolution of 1905 was about and Paris was inundated by very wealthy expatriates. These rich people wanted to have foods they were familiar with from their home lands. It was a very exciting time in our kitchens. Escoffier had continued to entrust me with more responsibilities and my love of cooking was only rivaled by my desires for Yasmina.

It ended up being after 1906 that sweet Yasmina returned from her journey to America. Something was different about her when we were finally able to spend some time alone. I attributed the changes to her time in new lands, meeting and observing interesting people.

On the very day Escoffier donned on me my chef's toque, I met with Yasmina. She held a small box. A gift for my accomplishment?

"Didier," her soft tones called to me, "I give to you on your fabulous day this temperature gauge for you to have and use always. The passion you have for your craft elevates you into the strata of true artist. The only thing you've demonstrated above your skills in the kitchen is the unconditional love given me these past wonderful years."

I opened the box she held out to me. Made of the finest coppers and brass, with a single precious stone inset in its dial face, this food thermometer was instantly the most cherished tool I would ever use.

"Wherever did you find such an amazing instrument?"

"My time with Miss Bevier was so illuminating. I observed and learned much from her. In addition to the scales she used from the company my father was investing in, she also entertained regularly a salesman from Taylor Instruments. This company is apparently one of America's leading thermometer manufacturers.

"Just a few months ago, Miss Bevier published her book 'Selection and Preparation of Food'. In it she proposes the use of a special kitchen thermometer in the roasting of meats. Didier, she carefully inserted a gauge directly into a thick roast and was able to know precisely when the food was cooked to perfection!

"It was her association with the thermometer representative, and I dare say what I'm sure was a developing love between the two, which led to her performing some amount of research and development of a new style of meat thermometer."

With all this news she shared, I had begun to detect the clouds of distress darkening her disposition.

"On such an amazing evening filled with gifts of love and affection and stories of amazement why are your eyes harboring such sadness, my beautiful one?"

It took Yasmina several moments to compose a reply. I was instantly transported back to that pantry, looking upon the face of that young woman filled with sadness and tears, sitting alone on a barrel.

"My dear Didier, this is more than a celebratory gift. It must also be my farewell token to you."

Surely she must be having a laugh at my expense. "I don't understand what you mean. How is this a farewell?"

"Because of your position in the kitchens, we've never been able to tell my father of our love. We both knew he would never except you. He has betrothed me to another; the son of a powerful and influential business partner."

Being beside myself, this news was more than I could bear. Slumping into a nearby chair, I begged of her, "But I've been granted the right to become a chef in my own restaurant. Surely your father will take that into consideration and permit me to ask for your hand in marriage?"

"It is too late, Didier. The business alliance which shall be created by my union with this man's son are more powerful forces than you and I can overcome. My father has commanded it. So shall it be."

If anything, Yasmina was completely devoted to her family and would never consider moving against the will of its patriarch. I knew this. It was just one of the many things that I loved so completely about her.

Aghast, Alayna looked upon the great chef's face observing that sadness had returned.

"I know that you never held her hand again, dearest cousin, for you have been completely devoted to the craft of creating your culinary delicacies since that time. I never knew what pain and sadness you've shouldered in your life."

"Thank you, fair Alayna. And you have born the brunt of a lifetime without the love and affection of a husband of your own. My eternal gratitude for all you have done for me since the end of the Great War."

Didier slumped further down into the bed. No longer able to see the Paris skyline, he clutches tightly to the temperature gauge, his words are soft. Alayna is barely able to understand what he says next or to whom he is speaking.

"I spent my life without your love. Unable to have you as my wife, my passion was spent striving to create the perfect meal which might elevate me above all others. This gauge you bestowed upon me magically kept your memories close to my heart in all the time we never had together. I swear to you, some day, in some way, your gift to me shall overcome that which divided us. Your gift will bridge the chasm between another chef's passion for perfection and loving his soul mate of destiny's design."

After those last, barely audible sounds, Didier's grip on the gauge loosened and it shifted slightly in his hand. Fearful of what she suspected Alayna's voice cried out.

"Didier? Didier? Where are you cousin? Surely you've not left me here alone?"

In that moment she realized the candle's reflection flickered no longer in the chef's dull, flat, lifeless eyes. As the temperature gauge altered its position in his hand, she thought she caught the candle's flame in the stone on its dial. With one hand she gently stroked down his face shutting his eyelids. With her other hand, as she removed Yasmina's gift from his grasp, the candle extinguished itself leaving but the Parisian city lights to illuminate the room.

Coming down the hall were the distinctive thumps of soldiers boots. Realizing she must have alerted them with her cries, she was immediately terrified. Suddenly, rapping on the door. Now fearing for her life, Alayna moved as fast as she could to face them.

The door opened such that the German officer outside could see Alayna as well as the dead old man in the bed. Perhaps it was the tears which streamed down her face, but the soldier immediately understood what had transpired. Without speaking, compassion flashed upon his face as he looked back from Didier and down upon Alayna. Placing a gloved index finger across his lips he encouraged her silence, eased the door shut, and led his troops down the hall.

3 GROWING UP

Gerald Anderson may have been tyrannical about his business and the way he ruled over wife and son, but results spoke for themselves. Having easily won the restaurant space from Raymond Walker, Gerald had set about to create a fine dining environment which would bring in customers able and willing to spend money for an exceptional evening out.

He had enlisted his wife's aid with much of the interior decoration of the lounge, bar, and dining areas. Though Betty's only training had come from the fine home she grew up in and those of her parent's friends and well to do family, she naturally had an eye for bringing symmetry and beauty to the spaces she created.

Greg continued to receive a steady flow of verbal abuse from his father. Add in the periodic beltings and what resulted was a boy who attempted to please his father but most often ended up disappointing. Greg had learned some time ago how to properly clean and dress himself, making sure to always represent the Anderson family with respect and honor.

As the summer of '83 approached, young Greg had finally turned 13. A teenager. While his mother was supportive of this hallmark in his life, the only other person he felt close enough to share his enthusiasm with was his best friend, Jeffrey Walker. In what had turned out to be a sort of ritual, someone from each family would make the trek across the street for the daily mail exchange. On this day it was the young boys.

"Hey Greg! What do you know?"

"I know that I'm no longer a baby, like you are Jeff Walker. Today I'm officially a teenager. Happy 13th birthday to me!"

"Wow. That's right. You don't look any cooler or anything. Maybe that happens tomorrow? Well, whenever it does, we'll have to celebrate. Maybe go to a movie or something?"

"Hey, I look cool. Cooler than you do, anyway. I've got another bill from that equipment delivery service for you. I thought your mother called and told them your address was one number less than ours? This is like the 3rd month in a row they've gotten it wrong."

Jeff had indeed overheard his mother talking with Harris Supplies, requesting they make the clerical correction.

"We called, we called. Grown ups are weird, so who knows what they do sometime. Hey, I'll trade you the electric bill at your dad's place for our delivery bill. You do want to have your night light on when you go to sleep, right?"

The boys had developed into fine friends since their parents bought those two empty eating establishments. Over the past six and a half years they walked to school together and were in the same grade. This allowed for the support of each others weaknesses when doing homework as they had all the same classes as well.

When they were allowed, much time was spent after classes and most of the summer simply gallivanting around the City, like kids do. But as they had gotten older Jeff seemed to have less time to hang out with his buddy. Instead, as his father would permit, he found himself tagging along in the kitchen almost literally hanging on his father's apron strings.

"What can I do for you this afternoon, Pop? I see a whole bunch of unpeeled potatoes over by the sink…"

Ray and Ruth had transformed what had been a nondescript eating space into something homey and casual. Unconsciously, they had found their target diners were families looking for a good value when going for an evening out. Producing the finest quality food was not always at the forefront of their efforts, however, the Walkers ensured their customers had a great time and returned as soon as possible.

Now nearly 17, Ray, Jr. had spent much of his free time helping the family by working in the kitchens. He resented being there.

"Come on, Pop. Do I really need to be here today cooking this slop for these people? There's an exciting world out there waiting to be explored and conquered."

"And how do you plan to finance your conquests, young man? Nothing comes for free, you know?"

Little Jeff chimed in, "Yeah, Junior, nothing is free."

Not wanting to be there, the words of his father and brother further irritated Ray, Jr. "Fine. I'm taking the day off. I'm not feeling well, Pop. Maybe you can squeeze some slave labor out of Jeff. I'm out of here."

Ray, Sr. knew his son was uncontrollable, and of his proclivity for getting into trouble.

"Look, Raymond, if you don't want to be here today, that's fine. Can you do your mother and I a favor, though? Can you stay out of trouble, please? We don't care for those boys you've been hanging around lately. Be a better example for your little brother. Jeffrey looks up to you. What do you say, kid?"

THE PERFECT MEAL

"Yeah, what do you say, kid?" Jeff was all smiles. He truly idolized his big brother. Perhaps it was only because Ray, Jr. was older and knew more about the world than Jeff.

"Whatever, Pop. You don't like any of my friends. That's cool. Whatever." He pushed Jeff out of his way as he left the kitchens through the back door.

"Hey, Junior. Cut it out, meanie!"

"Let him go, Jeff. Don't worry, he'll be back when his money runs out. Hey, we have work to do young man." Ray was still that jovial, fun loving father. "Hmmm. Well, I'm not quite sure how much production I'm going to get out of a one armed bandit. Have you learned how to hold a potato in one hand and the peeler in one of your feet?"

With that Ray stuck out his tongue at Jeff, nodded towards the massive pile of potatoes and told his son to quit slacking off and get his butt in gear.

"One day I may just have to teach myself that trick. You'll be sorry then, Pop!"

------ oOo ------

Gerald had always considered it somewhat of an irony that he had, in so many ways, followed his father's footsteps by getting into the food industries business. Growing up, working in his granddad's deli was fine until the day he'd nearly cut off his left thumb.

Both his grandfather and father had been in the back alley helping to unload supplies when the man at the counter demanded his sandwich be made for him.

"If you'd be so kind as to wait a few moments sir, some one will surely be back to help you. If you'd like, I would be most happy to start your order."

Young Gerry had the man's bread lying there with his requested condiments applied. Unfortunately, they were out of the meat requested and Gerry had never been allowed to handle a knife up to that point. After a few moments the man threatened to leave. He would buy his food elsewhere.

The last thing Gerry wanted was to get in trouble for a half finished sandwich on the counter when his father returned. Never shy to try new things, he figured it could not be all that hard to slice some meat and finish the job. Imagine how proud his elders would be when they saw how he had handled the order in their absence.

Unfortunately, there was some training and skill the boy should have received. The customer was no help in the matter either. Pressuring Gerry that the amount of meat was not worth the price, Gerry went for more, but the knife slid off a bone hidden to his view, and sliced deeply into his left thumb.

The customer left in disgust as Gerry's father and grandfather rushed up to the counter to witness the bloody mess.

As Gerald thought back on that day, he caught himself rubbing the long scar on his left hand. He had actually been quite lucky. Just a few centimeters the other way, no use of his left thumb at all.

------ oOo ------

Greg was passing by his father's open office door with a baseball glove in hand. He was a bit bummed that Jeff was not going to be joining him for a catch this afternoon, but knew he would have fun with whomever he came across at the field.

Catching sight of his son passing, Gerald called out to him.

"Greg, I'd like you to help out in the kitchen today. We've just had to let go of another dishwasher and there's just been no time to get him replaced. Hopefully tomorrow or the next day I'll be able to hire someone new. Until then, you need to help out."

"Aw, dad!" exclaimed the now dejected boy. He knew it was absolutely pointless to even begin to argue his case for getting out into nature, breathing clean fresh air, and honing his athletic skills.

"Damn it, Greg, enough of your attitude. Do you think that baseball and mitt came free of charge? The clothes on your back and the food I feed you every day is all paid for because of the hard work I do at this restaurant. I am sick and tired of you acting like a baby. Now, unless you are feeling up to a session with me and a belt, I suggest you dismiss that attitude of yours and get ready for lunch service.

"Besides son, you have to work your way up in the kitchen if you're ever going to be accepted to the best culinary school in France. You need to learn every station. Understand exactly what is going on with every aspect of the meal's preparation. One of the main reasons your mother and I invested in this business was to give you every opportunity. We have sacrificed a lot for you."

"Yes, I know father. I know."

"If I'd not had that kitchen accident when I was about your age now, who knows where I might have gone in the ranks of great chefs. But someone has to run the business and in this family, that someone is me. Besides, your mother loves you very much and believes you are going to be the best chef of all time. Now put away that ball glove, get your apron on, and help out in the kitchen. I'll check on you in a bit."

"Yes, father," was all Greg was able to muster as he turned to go. The spring in his step had turned into something approaching a dead man walking. His father used that story about nearly cutting off his thumb as a kid so many times that it lost its sense of legitimacy. Greg had never noticed his father unable to perform a task with his left hand. Perhaps this was what they referred to as a life lesson.

4 BIRTH AND DEATH

Given their close geographic proximity, Jeff considered Greg to be his best friend. There had not been many other every day companions growing up. Only a few of the shops on their street had livable spaces above them. Fewer still had families with children their age. So it usually came down to the two young boys getting together and exploring their neighborhood. Both of their mothers had forbid them from going to far away. Though times were getting better with respect to crime, they did not live in a perfect world.

For whatever reason Ray, Jr. seemed to be able to get away with more transgressions against his parents. Unfortunately this tended to have the effect of the more Ray got away with the more he wanted to get away with. His father tended to be more dismissive of Junior's actions, however Ruth was not afraid of making her feelings known to the young man.

"Raymond, Jr., I am talking to you. Come back her. Right now."

Knowing this conversation was likely to be long and drawn out, Ray had tried to sneak out the back door of the kitchen before his mother could launch into whatever scolding tirade she had planned.

"Going to be late, Mom. Need to meet up with my friends. We have plans, you know."

"No, young man, I do not know. You still have not explained to me where you were until after 2 a.m. last night. Why are you constantly pushing the envelope with regards to the rules your father and I have laid out for you? Are we such strict totalitarians that you cannot possibly find your way to do what we ask. Jeffrey doesn't seem to have a problem following our few, simple rules. What are we going to do about you, Raymond?"

"Mom, Jeff is a little kid. Of course he's going to do every little thing you ask. I did the same when I was his age. But I'm grown up now, and there are far more interesting and exciting things to do in this city and the world than hang out on this block until I turn 25. Lighten up, will ya? Geesh."

"I will lighten up when you start behaving in a respectable manner. You are going to get yourself involved in something terrible one of these days. And when that happens who do you suppose you are going to come crying to for help? Do you really think your friends are going to be around when the going gets tough? Well?"

"You're as bad as Pop with the trash talking about my friends. Get off my back, will you? We are just out for a good time. What the hell is wrong with that? Didn't you have a good time when you were my age? Can you even remember that long ago?"

Ordinarily Ruth might have found that question humorous, however it angered her this time.

"That is not a very polite thing to say to your mother, young man. Unless you decide to start behaving better, and now, your father and I will have no other choice but to ground you. Then you'll be stuck exploring the way from your bedroom down here to the dishwasher and back to your room."

Ruth was unable understand what had gotten into her oldest boy. She did not like the changes he was exhibiting towards the family or the shirking of his responsibilities. Thinking a change of tact in her approach might work better, she softened her tone and implored to him once more.

"Junior, won't you please let go of this craziness consuming your life? Is everything your father and I have provided you really that bad? I know we may not have the finest things, but you boys have always had a roof, good food, clothes, shoes. Sure we ask for your help from time to time, but that's nothing more strenuous than doing chores for an allowance. Could you please just start coming home on time and taking care of the work your father needs here in the restaurant?"

Seeing a way out of her verbal hell, Ray, Jr. decided to tell her what she needed to hear in order to release him. "Yes, of course Mother. I hear what you are saying, and I'll do everything I can not to be out late. But I really need to go now. My friends are waiting for me out back and I don't want to hold them up any longer."

She doubted his sincerity. Watching him leave, Ruth felt the sadness inside her grow a bit more vast as the door clicked shut. They definitely grew up too fast. At least little Jeffrey was going to be there, ever so compliant and eager to please, for a while longer. Those thoughts brought a smile to her face. For a brief moment, at least.

"HEY MOM!" shouted the object of her mental interlude. Jeff had sneaked up behind his mother while she day dreamed. In his hands were several letters which he planned on taking over to the Anderson's place.

THE PERFECT MEAL

"Why you little devil you. I'm going to have to spank you for scaring me like that. Come here young man. I have something for you."

Though he knew his mother was joking with him, letting her catch him was out of the question at his age. "No can do, Mother, oh Mother of mine. I am on my daily chore of swapping mail with Greg. You told me just the other day how important it is to make sure I do this every day, so you will understand that I cannot allow for a spanking to delay my chores. Unless of course what you told me was not true. Were you lying to me oh Mother dear?"

Hearing him speak like that forced her to smile even in light of her verbal sparring session with his brother. "Young man, you go about your appointed rounds. Neither rain, nor snow, nor a mother scared to death shall keep you from properly delivering your mail. Off with you. But make sure you don't wander off, do you hear?"

"Yes, Mother dear. I hear and obey." Having watched too many creature feature movies, Jeff walked stiff legged away from his mother with both arms stretched out in front of him, as if in a trance.

Not one to miss out on a perfectly good opportunity, Ruth reached for a nearby towel, balled it up and called to her son, "Oh, Jeffrey Walker. You forgot something dear son of mine."

By the time she had finished speaking his name the towel was speeding towards the boy's head. He received it with perfect timing as he turned back to face his mother.

"Awe, Mom!"

Mid afternoon and no one was around the front of Anderson's place. Jeff was very quiet when he opened the front door and was able to slip inside without causing the bells to jingle. He had worked very hard to be able to perform such stealthy feats. He dropped off the few pieces of mail onto the hostess stand and skirted his way around the edge of the restaurant to the side entrance which led one to either the kitchen, the back offices or the stairway to the flats above. Still undetected, Jeff vaulted upwards two stairs at a time, but making his way along the far left edge where at his family's place he had discovered the left side of the stairs were much less squeaky than the middle or right.

Once he got to the front door of the residence, he decided to just try the knob. He had made it that far without detection, so why not try and sneak all the way into Greg's room. Surely his best friend would be impressed if he were able to pull it off. Greg's dad would be working downstairs, so Jeff only had to contend with Mrs. Anderson.

Slowly opening the front door, a quick survey through the crack revealed the front room empty. Quietly, he closed the door and made the short trip down the hallway. Greg's room was the last on the right, his parents had the room opposite. Inching his way forward he noticed Mrs. Anderson on the bed in her room. Not normally a voyeur, he had to stop for a moment and stare. The shades had been drawn so only a minimal amount of light was streaming inside. What illumination was there lit Betty's body in all the right places. Jeff was not sure if she was sleeping since her head was turned away from his vantage point in the hall. He was sure that her robe was open and slivers of light were dancing on her breasts, mid-section and across her hips. The panties she wore seemed moist in the area visible thanks to her thighs having been spread apart several inches.

Jeff had seen his mother in her undergarments before, but never had quite experienced this. Whether it was the sneaking into their apartment, Betty's theatrical setting or the strange yet wonderful sensations he had while watching her, when Greg jerked open his door Jeff nearly jumped two feet up and back away from his friend.

"Get in here, Jeff. What are you doing? How long have you been here?" All spoken in hushed tones by the slightly older boy.

Even though they were now inside and Greg had gently closed his bedroom door, Jeff replied in hushed tones, "Just snuck in Greg. I made it from the front door all the way to your bedroom without anyone seeing me. Not even you mother. I'm the best!"

Pride in his accomplishments prevented Jeff from noticing his friend was somewhat distracted. The looks of concern on Greg's face came through in his tone of voice. "Hey, that's great, man. You're the best."

Finally, Jeff figured out something was bothering Greg. Expecting something to be broken, he looked around the room. "Everything all right? You don't seem very excited about what I did. Oh, are you in trouble for something? What did you do this time, Greg?"

"We're friends, right Jeff? Best friends, right?"

"I hope so. I just broke into your restaurant and apartment without worrying what would happen to me if I got caught. I'd say I trust you as a best friend. Do you consider me your best friend, too?"

"Of course. I trust you too. I really want to tell you something but don't want you to think I'm weird and start hating me or anything. Can I tell you what happened this morning? You have to promise that you will never, ever, ever tell anyone else. Promise?"

"Promise, Greg. I promise. What happened?"

"I don't want to be gross or anything, but have you ever woke up and found your sheets wet, but you didn't pee the bed?"

"Uhm, no. But my big brother told me about that. I think he called them wet dreams or something. Of course, he started calling me a wet dream after that so I figure it can't be all that good. Why?"

"Okay, well, just remember, you promised. I woke up this morning and my pajamas and sheets were all wet and sticky. I really wasn't sure what had happened, but knew that if my father found out, he would not be very happy with me."

"Oh, yeah. I remember those last couple of times you told me about him whipping you for having peed the bed. But that was a long time ago."

"I know. But my father is not very forgiving about stuff like that, so I didn't want to tell him. Instead, after he had gone downstairs to work, I called for my mother. I wanted to ask her if she would help me keep it from him."

Greg proceeded to share what happened after his mother had seen him and the bed. For as long as he could remember, she had always been there to provide the love and support he needed after receiving a belt from his father for not performing up to some lofty standard. He felt very close to her. But this felt like something different.

"I told my mother that just before I woke up I remembered having a dream about being with her in a giant bed. We didn't have on any clothes and I was laying on top of her."

"Wow. Really? Was that like weird to you? I don't think I've ever had a dream like that."

"I guess so. But what I remember of the dream, it wasn't strange to me at all. In fact, by the time I woke up I have to say it was pretty awesome. Then I realized things were all messed up in my bed, and I was back to being weirded out."

"So what did you mother do when you told her? Did you tell her?"

Greg had told Betty about his dream. Her response was in line with all the other motherly love and support she had expressed to him.

"It is perfectly natural for you to have dreams about me that way, Gregory. I was the one who gave birth to you and brought you into this world. There have been times over the years I too have had similar dreams about us being so close together. Don't worry about anything, dear. Would you like me to help you understand what was happening with your body during all of this?"

He did, and so she talked with him about his growth and maturity. He was becoming a man, and this dream was simply one of the ways nature used to convey that knowledge. They sat on Greg's bed and as the two discussed various aspects of the early morning events, Betty began to experience familiar sensations of her own.

The gentle touching and caressing she had begun her explanations with eventually turned into more. There was nothing Greg could do about the way his body responded to her touch. Eventually he found she was discussing the physical attributes associated with what had caused him to ejaculate during his dreams. It occurred to her that now was the perfect time to have that talk about sex with her teenager.

Greg continued asking his mother pointed questions about erections, intercourse, and various other aspects of love making. The longer the discussion continued the more aroused they both became.

"Mother!" Betty had finally succumbed to her feelings of desire and slipped a hand into his shorts. Her stroking caused him to focus completely on the actions at hand.

"It's okay, Greg. This is perfectly normal. It is how you will learn to please and love a woman." She helped him lay back and started to kiss him gently on the lips while maintaining the position and motion of her hand.

Greg was completely back in that dream state with little cognizance of his mother having removed his shorts. Pulling his naked body on top of her, she gently guided him inside. At nearly 41 years old, she still had amazing legs which she firmly wrapped around his waist, pulling him in deeper. This was all remarkably similar to his dream, he was still on that large bed making love to her. As his mouth surrounded Betty's nipples, an urgency began to mount inside and within a few moments it was over.

Gently allowing the boy to slip off her prone body, Betty quietly left him there on his bed, alone and asleep. She made her way to the room she shared with Gerald and closed the blinds most of the way. It was only moments until her relaxed body and mind was asleep in the filtered rays of early afternoon sun. It was perhaps only a few moments more that young Jeff Walker was admiring the view from outside her doorway.

------ oOo ------

Jeff would always remember that early morning in September, 1983. His bedroom window was at the very back of the building which housed his family's restaurant and apartments. His view was nothing spectacular, though it did provide complete, unobstructed sight lines up and down the alleyway.

The noise of car motors reverberated off the building walls and into his bedroom. It was the rotating lights of the police and ambulance vehicles bouncing off his walls which awoke him fully. With his head sticking out the window, he saw his mother and father talking with a uniformed officer near the back entrance of their kitchen. Quickly dressing himself, he ran down the stairs making his way through the kitchen and to the alley.

He was still on the slight side and had no problem slipping past the officer posted at the back door. Quietly making his way behind his parents, he listened to their conversation with the man who appeared to be in charge.

"So you heard some shouting, and recognized one of the voices as belonging to your son, uhm," he fumbled a page or two back through his notebook.

"Raymond Walker, Jr.," Jeff heard his mother say.

THE PERFECT MEAL

"Uhm, yes. And then what did you do?"

The elder Ray spoke up. "We put on some clothes and made our way down here to see what the commotion was all about. Before we actually got outside, we heard what I think were gunshots and as we opened the back door, a car was tearing off down the alley."

"And you didn't catch a glimpse of the make? Model? Not even the license plate number? Anything? Did you see anything or anyone else that might have been involved?"

Ruth and Ray's heads were bowed, staring at the ground. "No, nothing. All we saw was Junior on the ground over there. It seemed there was a pool of blood around him." Ray was reliving the moment of discovery in his mind. As he did, he noticed Jeff had been listening. Looking up at his wife, he turned and the two of them pulled Jeffrey, now their only son, closer.

Flipping closed his notepad, the policeman in charged shared condolences, "We'll do everything in our power to figure this out, Mr. and Mrs. Walker. I'll keep in touch. In case you discover something new you should share it with us." He handed them a business card, turned and left the three of them huddling together in their early morning grief.

Later that morning, when Betty brought over some postal items to the Walker's she was excited about some news she could hardly wait to share with her good friend, Ruth. Entering the front of the restaurant, the only person Betty could find was a line cook who had come in early to begin preparing for the lunch service. He directed her to the residence upstairs. She could tell something was not right, and her excitement was

diminishing with every step. Ruth answered Betty's knock at the door, and the sadness emanating from the apartment washed over the visitor.

"Thank you so much for coming over, Betty. I would have called you sooner, but this is overwhelming. So overwhelming."

Listening to the news of what became of Ray, Jr. was completely unexpected. In addition to bringing over errant mail, the real reason Betty had popped over that morning was to share with the Walkers she and Gerald's good news. Now, however seemed absolutely the worse time to tell friends who had suddenly lost a child that her family was expecting a new one of their own.

5 CULINARY DREAMS

One could hardly refer to them as boys anymore. Greg and Jeff, a year and a half out of high school, had matured into lovely young men. Like their fathers, both of them were on the competitive side. Whether running like the wind to catch a missed bus or attempting to show the other up chopping vegetables in the kitchen, one would not label these fellows as slow and lazy.

They were strapping. Handsome, with almost rugged figures. Jeff had longer, sandy blond hair which just grazed his wide shoulders, until his father was after him to tie it up and keep it out of the patron's dinner plates. At just over 6' tall, he had a presence which commanded confidence and authority.

That strong personality came with a tinge of arrogance which some might call over-confidence. Much of his formative years had been spent in the kitchen wielding knives, pots and pans. Jeff was well adjusted to the cooking life.

Having innate cooking talent combined with quite the versatile palate had raised his profile with co-workers as well as awards committee of several youth cooking competitions. The more accolades bestowed upon him, the harder he worked. This was something which pleased Ray immensely. Although Jeff's parents had tried pushing him away from a life in the kitchen, in fact, even trying to implant the idea of going to school out on the West Coast in order to get a real feel for the country. They had wanted to move him away from the same influences which had ultimately killed Ray, Jr.

One of the reasons the Walkers changed their mind came in March of 1984 after Gerald and Betty had their new baby. The Andersons had asked Ray and Ruth to be godparents to Lizbeth. Accepting that responsibility helped soften the Walkers attitude about continuing to make New York City their home.

THE PERFECT MEAL

Over the ensuing years, Ruth spent a fair share of her time looking over Lizbeth which left Raymond to care for Jeff. The best way for him to do that was to have Jeff help him out in some way in the kitchens. That on-the-job babysitting had paid off by producing a young man eager and willing to do some hard work in order to make meal service as good as possible. Knowing his son was unlikely to shirk the responsibilities of a good day of labor, Ray had no problems asking him for help when the staff got behind.

"Jeff, I need you to help the sous chef with his mis en place. I've been working with him all day on new specials for the menu and it seems he's not able to chat with me and cut veggies here in the kitchen at the same time."

"Obviously he never had to grow extra arms as a child. No problems, Pop. I've got you both covered."

Never one to shy away from getting noticed for his effort and ability, Jeff jumped right into the sous chef's station to get everything set up and ready for the evening meal. There was something extremely pleasurable about this preparation time in the kitchen. As much as he loved the actual rush which occurred when orders started flooding in, it was this gentle calm before the storm which provided the mental rest and recharging one needed before entering into the fray of things.

Jonny, one of the longest employed line cooks at the Walker's restaurant was working at the station opposite of Jeff.

"So, when's it happening, kid? When you flying this joint and heading off to fancy Francy?"

"It won't be soon enough to get away from you, Jonny. Hey, do you smell that? What is that? Are you wearing cologne again? Wait, that's not, oh! Did you have fish gut duty again?" Jeff starts laughing, holding his nose in exaggerated fashion with his elbow above his head. Having spent a lot of time in between the various jokes, insults, and occasional verbal sparring sessions, Jeff knows how to both dish it out and take it in the heat of the kitchen.

"Okay, kid. Yuck it up. But wait until the next time you have fish prep. I'll make sure your old man comes up with the idea, all on his own, that we should have an all seafood special day. You'll be scrubbing stink off you for weeks."

The good natures between most of the kitchen staff was one of the reasons Jeff spent much of his teenage years helping out. Greg might have been his best friend, but his father was truly his hero in life. His parents had started this business with every penny of money they owned in the world and had slowly built a wonderful foundation and in the process a great life for a kid. At least from his perspective. Money was never free flowing, but he'd never done without the essentials. While his culinary school education fund had been raided a few times for business emergencies, he just about had enough to cover all his expenses for the trip there, 2 years of advanced training, and perhaps even a little fun if time permitted it. Going to learn from the best France had to offer was something he had dreamed about since first watching Emerill Lagasse on that new Food Network several years ago. It was Emerill and his "BAM" tag line that got him excited about some day having his own cooking shows and having aspiring cooks shouting whatever his personal kitchen slogan ended up being.

"BAM!" Jeff shouted as he sunk the cleaver he had been working with into the cutting board. Perhaps it was the volume of the sudden explosion of knife and voice which caused Jonny to jump a bit.

"Ha ha ha! Made you flinch! You flinched. Drinks are on you tonight, Jonny!"

"Little brat! I had something all planned for you later. Well, don't turn you back tomorrow, kid. I will get you back. Whenever you leave for school can't be soon enough."

"I haven't even gotten accepted yet, man. I've been working my butt off reading through Escoffier's and Joel Robuchon's classic cookbooks. I just finished the Culinary Institute of America textbook by McGee 'On Food and Cooking'. For the second time."

"Isn't that like 800 pages? Wow, maybe you're not as dumb as you look after all," Jonny smiled as he watched Jeff unravel the backhanded compliment.

"If all goes well, I should hopefully hear from the school in the next few weeks. Then I'll be leaving to enter their program in the early fall. I can hardly wait. And even though I won't miss your ugly mug at all, I will miss hanging around with all you bums around here."

Ray was entering the kitchen with his sous chef and caught that last bit from Jeff, "Bums here in the kitchen, eh? Don't make me remind you that your mother and I had to wrestle more than one bum in the past in order to retrieve a lost arm or leg you allowed to slip away with no regard for your own well being."

"Ah, Pop. You know I have super human abilities to grow new body parts on command. I don't know why you try and hold that over me now that I'm all grown up. Besides when was the last time you had a bum fight on my behalf? Seems to me that you did get into an argument with old Sammy out back because he didn't want you locking up the dumpster."

Looking at the now almost completely healed bruises around his elder's eye, he asked, "Remind us all how that one went for you, Champ?"

The other line cooks and employees moving about the kitchen burst into laughter. Not wanting to miss out on the good times, Ruth passed through the kitchen doors as she heard the uproar coming from the prep stations.

THE PERFECT MEAL

Dropping a folder on a nearby table she asked her husband, "Ray, honey? Do you need me to get you another bag of ice for your eye? We don't want permanent damage you know."

Even more laughter. Being of relatively good nature, Ray faked getting mad.

"Everyone with a smile on their faces right now is fired!" he shouted. "I don't care how much you all like Sammy. In fact, why don't all you laughers head on out back and join him right now!"

As if responding to cue, cooks put down their knives, dishwashers tossed soapy rags, and Ruth proceeded to lead everyone out of the kitchen in a comic exodus at the behest of their boss.

"Okay, okay. Just because I'm a salt of the earth kind of guy, and against my better judgment, I'll rehire you all to your former positions. There will be a 10% reduction in salary, and extra unpaid shifts for all of you rascals this summer as well. This is my final offer."

No one stopped and turned around until Ruth paused to get some clarity from her husband.

"Does that mean we'll still be going on vacation this summer, Ray?"

"Other than hellfire and brimstone keeping us away, only if we have a full kitchen staff to look after things while we are in the Bahama's, oh beautiful wife of mine," he winked back at her.

"Okay. You heard the man. Get back to your stations. And get with it. Look alive. Let's make dinner magic happen!"

Through the mock verbal disgruntlement the staff shuffled themselves back into their positions. From the other side of the room someone shouted, "We're only coming back 'cause we don't like Sammy's cologne." More laughter still.

This was exactly what Jeff enjoyed about his parents, and especially the way they treated the folks who worked so hard to make their business a success. He would always be grateful and have much respect for what they had done with their lives. The restaurant business was tough. Margins always tight. But it was his life. A good life. One he loved.

The same genial attitude was not something which had been cultivated in the kitchen of the Anderson's restaurant. Even though Gerald did not spend much time in the heat of things, he ruled the staff and atmosphere with an iron glove. The budding chef who had initially invested in the restaurant had come and gone in the matter of just a couple of years as a result of the endless reprimands handed down by Gerald.

Greg often pondered how his father treated people in general, but especially those under his employ. The elder Anderson carried a somewhat elitist attitude towards those he felt beneath him on the socioeconomic ladder. More than once Greg covered someones job duties because Gerald had taken to firing the employee. The good thing about such predicaments was there was nothing in the kitchen, or the whole restaurant for that matter, which Greg was unable to do. Having greeted more people at the front door than a semi-retired worker in Walmart, he knew all the tricks of the trade when it came to washing dishes in a professional kitchen; and pretty much everything in between.

Of course, none of these skills and abilities made him overly thrilled with the prospect of spending the rest of his life in the hospitality industry. Yes, his father and father's father had been working in or owning some sort of eatery all the way back to the early 20th century. But this was modern times, and Greg felt there had to be something more exciting and interesting than slaving away in a kitchen.

Like Jeff, Greg was a ruggedly handsome young man. His growth spurt had tapered off leaving him at 5'11". His father required of all the kitchen staff to maintain short, clean haircuts. Greg was no exception.

The birth of his little sister had the positive effect for him of dominating most of his mother's time and energy. There had never been another encounter between them, but the way she looked at male customers made him wonder as to her motives.

Gerald, at an extreme end of the discipline spectrum had been counter balanced by Betty's emotive love and over caring. Caught in the middle was Greg. He found it difficult to seek fatherly advice and just as soon would leave his mother's words of wisdom for Lizbeth's ears.

The more Betty inquired as to the status of his school admission, the more Greg pushed back.

"Mother, please quit nagging me about that darned application already. I sent it in months ago and still haven't heard back from the selection committee. Maybe I'm just not good enough to get trained by the best culinary minds in France. I'm sure there is something equally as tragic that I might get myself involved with."

"Gregory Anderson you are an excellent prospect for that school. You can chop and saute and souffle with the very best young cooks."

"Of course I can Mother. But what if that's not what I want to do for the rest of my life. That's forever, you know?"

"Honey, what would your father think? Your grandfather would roll over in his grave if he thought his precious, only grandson didn't want to carry on the family tradition. Besides, you want to go to France with your friend, Jeff, and have a wonderful couple of years as you both train to be master chefs, don't you?"

Those were more his parents desires. He liked Jeff a lot, and definitely considered him a best friend. But the past few years, and especially since school let out, Jeff had increased the amount of time he spent in his father's kitchens. This resulted in less hanging out and just kicking around like they did throughout high school.

"Jeff lives and breathes food and cooking. I can appreciate his passion, but I'm just not at that same level of dedication to the career."

"Well, whatever else would you like to do, dear?"

"I don't know. Maybe I could just kick around Europe for a couple of years and find myself and figure out what I want?"

"And how do you think that request is going to go over with your father? You know we have been working to build this business to be able to turn it over to you one day. The only way he's ever going to retire and hand you the reins is if you get the training and prove to him you have the ability to take his life's work and build upon it. He just wants the best for you, dear. We both want you to succeed and do well in life."

As mother and son were sitting alone in their apartment kitchen, Betty reached out to take hold of his hand. Flinching at her action, Greg jerked his hand away from her. He had not permitted her to touch him in many years.

In the silence which built up between them, Greg came to a decision.

"Perhaps you are right, Mother. Maybe I really do want to get away. I think I've had enough of the local sights and sounds. Be sure to let Father know how excited I am to get the good news about school."

Betty watched her son leave the room. She was somber in the realization he may have just left her forever.

6 ADMISSIONS LETTER

As had been the case so many times, the Anderson's needed another line cook for their lunch and dinner services. Greg had already been forcibly recruited by his father, however they were still one man down.

During their morning coffee klatch Betty requested if Jeff might be available for kitchen duty that day.

"Oh, Ruth. You know how hard headed Gerry can be. Instead of biding time and planning ahead, he just continually fires his employees on the spot. Last week it was right in the middle of dinner."

"Really? How were you all able to finish the service?"

Betty, a bit disgusted, but with the slightest tinge of self-satisfaction, "Well, if you can believe it, Mr. Know-It-All actually had to jump into the mix and give the cooks a hand."

"What about his bad thumb?"

"Oh, he tried to play that card, trust me, Ruth. Trust me. But he knew they would never get out of the weeds. So, he sucked it up and worked through. Of course the fellow hired to replace the previous guy only lasted until last night. And now, we need more. Do you think Jeff would be willing and able to come over for lunch and dinner? I know Greg would appreciate having a friend nearby."

"He's absolutely able, Betty. Willing? Well, that's another matter. Don't you worry, I'll have him over by 11 a.m."

"Ruth I don't know where we'd be if you and I weren't such good friends. If only our husbands could get over their egos and remove their heads from their, well you know from where." Betty didn't often talk like this out loud. Clearly she thought along those lines from time to time.

THE PERFECT MEAL

Ruth chuckled partly from Betty's near comment and partly at how out of character it had been for her to make.

"Ever since you asked Ray and I to be Lizabeth's god parents, I just knew we would be close friends for a long, long time. Even if you did only ask us because of what happened to Ray, Jr. We girls have to stick together. Don't worry, those bull heads we call our husbands will come around sooner or later."

"Let's just hope it's sooner."

Betty left the Walker's dining room as Ruth cleared their coffee cups and cake plates. Passing into the kitchen on her way back to the dish washing area she noticed Jeff at the stove.

"What are you teaching yourself today, dear?"

Intently reading a passage from an older thick cookbook, Jeff didn't register his mother was speaking to him.

"AHEM! Hello. Earth to egg flipping young man. Anyone home?"

By this time she had moved into his peripheral vision and it was this motion which startled him into responding.

"Oh! Hello mother. Why are you sneaking up on people? Don't you know how dangerous that can be in the kitchen? Are you trying to make me burn my eyebrows off or something?"

How many times had Ruth seen her son doing these sort of extra curricular activities early in the morning before her husband or the rest of the staff made it to work? Just another aspect of the hard work and dedication she loved so much about him.

"Yes, silly boy. You know how much I despise bushy eyebrows on men. My only motivation was to provide you with proper grooming. How will you ever find someone to love you with all that stuff growing above your eyes?"

Jeff simply stuck out his tongue at her and smiled as he rolled the omelet out of the pan and onto a plate.

"Well just for that young man, I am banishing you from our kitchens for the day."

He stopped and stared at her.

"And since you now have nothing to do here, I would take it as a personal favor if you'd go across the street and give your friend Greg a hand with lunch and dinner."

"Mom! Really? Aw, come on. You know I was just playing with you. If I promise to never stick my tongue at you again, will you let me stay? Please. Pretty please?"

"Does that promise include shaving off those bushy eyebrows as well?" Her mischievous look teased him even more.

Defeated and over acting in complete deadpan, "What time do they want me to be there, oh mother dear?"

"If you could be there by 11 A.M. you would be helping them out a lot. Mr. Anderson is having trouble filling positions and has recruited Greg as well."

Jeff didn't mind the prospect of hanging with his friend, and always enjoyed working in the kitchen, but just being that close to the elder Anderson gave him the shivers.

"Somehow I'm beginning to think I've been set up here, mother dear. I should have held out for a better deal."

"There is always next time Jeffrey. Thanks honey. You are the best, right?"

His only reply was to jut his head out towards his mother, chin first and with contrived effort stick his tongue out as far is it would stretch. The image he created was so comical, Ruth could only laugh at him. She also managed to toss an uneaten biscotti towards the caricature's head.

Gerald appreciated promptness in his staff and always respected the young Walker for showing up before it was time for work to kick off. This wasn't the first time Jeff had filled in at Anderson's. Given Gerald's ways it likely would not be the last. If nothing else had transpired over the years between the heads of the two families it was a sincere respect that the business was what allowed them to provide for their families.

Going around to the employee's entrance was quite a bit out of Jeff's way, but he knew Mr. Anderson. Staying off his radar as long as possible was always a worthy goal. Coming in from the back, however, he had to pass by the open office door.

"Good morning, sir. I was hoping to hang out with Greg today and thought I might offer you some extra hands on the line, but only if I might be able to contribute."

Jeff knew this had all been arranged, but one of the lessons his father had taught him early in life was always attempt to allow the other person to think they are in control of the situation. It would have been very easy to have left Gerald with the impression that a favor was being bestowed upon him.

"Do you think you're up for Garde Manager, Jeff? If so, I might be able to squeeze you in for the day. By tomorrow I should have someone new hired and ready to take over that station. Ask Greg to get you a clean apron."

Bending his head back towards the paperwork neatly stacked on his desk, Gerald went about his work. Jeff smiled to himself as he walked on towards the kitchen. He found Greg busy working on prepping food at his station for the lunch shift.

"Hey Jeff. My mom mentioned you were going to help us out today. You have no idea how thankful I am to be working next to you and not my father. Again."

This time, Jeff smiled outwardly and gave a little laugh, "Dude, your pop isn't that bad. Come on."

"You should have been here last night when he fired that guy. Ouch. Hey, have you heard anything about getting into school? If they don't let us know soon, my folks are going to drive me completely insane."

Laughing again, "Nothing on my side of the street yet either, but it has to be soon if they expect us to actually get there in time for classes to start."

"Seriously. What do you think they are going to tell us? I know you are going to get in no problem. All Mr. Dedicated to everything food related."

"Right, right. That's me. Nothing on my agenda but food, food, food. Man, you are one of the best on the line I've seen over here or back in our kitchens. You're in like Flynn."

"For my parents sake, I certainly hope so. You'd think it was them leaving to go have fun and frolic in France for two years. But I tell you what, I'm really getting to the point that if I don't go, somewhere, soon, I'm not sure what I'm going to do."

"Somehow I'm sure there's going to be less frolicking and more fooding while we're there. Besides, with your family's reputation in the business, you are more likely to go than I am."

"At this point, I really hope so, Jeff. When they first started talking about all this cooking school stuff, it was so far away. Now, it's right around the corner. Plus, I really need to get away from the folks. You know what I mean? Just need a break."

Jeff really did not have those same urges to flee his home life. Though it was rough right after his brother died, his folks finally supported his culinary dreams. His attitude towards the future and that of his family business changed when his parents started supporting him.

"The thing I'm looking forward to Greg, is that deep dive into hands on training. Even though I've learned tons reading, practicing, and working in our kitchens, there is so much more. Can you imagine how good we'll both be when we're done? And when I get back home one of the first things I hope to do is start upgrading our place. My Pop has poured his heart and soul into making the business prosper. It just seems to me the next logical step is to kick things up a notch and move operations to the next level."

"I hear what you are saying. I really wish I had the same excitement about a future in this racket that you do. All I know is my folks are all jacked up on this concept of me going, becoming a master chef and then spending the rest of my natural life in this very kitchen. Only difference is that I'll be standing about 6 feet in that direction."

Greg pointed towards the main stove where the Executive Chef station was. Jeff turned in that direction and as was typical responded, "There are worse stations in life. Have you ever met Sammy out in our back alley? If so, you know what I mean."

Anderson's was moderately busy for the lunch service and very little interaction occurred between Greg and Jeff which was not work related. Just after the chef had called for the brigade to shut things down, Mr. and Mrs. Anderson came into the kitchen.

"Honey, would you and Jeff mind coming into the dining area for a moment? We have a surprise for you both." Greg thought he knew what his mother was referring to as he looked in Jeff's direction. Jeff was thinking the same.

Busboys were cleaning the last dishes from the empty tables. Greg and Jeff noticed the Walkers were there also. Mr. and Mrs. Anderson moved to join them, the two wives standing between their husbands. Betty and Ruth were holding envelopes which seemed from the perspective of the young men to have the same logo. Betty spoke first.

"We know you hard working, brilliant young chefs have been waiting a long, long time to find out the culinary school's decision."

Jeff and Greg had been thinking correctly. This was it. Jeff could hardly wait to find out that they were accepted and would be heading off to France in a couple of months. Ruth began the process of carefully unsealing the letter, not wanting to rip it or otherwise mar this pivotal moment in her son's life.

Instead of removing the letter she leaned over and whispered into Betty's ear. The two mothers conferred, smiled, and approached their sons.

Betty spoke, "Boys, this is your moment. You should be the ones to read us your acceptance letters." She handed Greg his, Ruth delivered Jeff's.

The weight of their future was now in the hands of the young men. Jeff thought to himself how heavy the ounce or two of his letter felt. For Greg, the reality of being able to fly away from life here was literally in the palm of his hands.

Looking up at their parents, neither Jeff nor Greg attempted to read the contents of their envelope. For his own reasons, each of them contemplated the anticipation of the coming news. To them time seemed to have stopped. For their parents, thirty seconds or so was long enough to wait.

Breaking the silence Ray spoke up, "All right you ham sandwiches. Stop milking the lime light. Get on with it. Spill the beans."

Jeff snapped out his trance first and elbowed Greg. The two looked at each other, then down at the envelopes. Pulling his folded letter out first, all eyes and ears awaited what Jeff had to say.

Instead of unfolding it, he shoved it into one of Greg's hands. "You read mine. I can't do it. Besides, it will be good luck."

Grinning, Greg swapped his letter with Jeff. "One. Two. Three."

THE PERFECT MEAL

Simultaneously they started reading to themselves the contents of what the culinary school had written to their best friend. Given the letter was only a single page it seemed to take them a long time to complete. Greg looked up First at Jeff, then towards his parents. Jeff's gaze followed that of his friend.

"Well?" inquired Gerald.

7 UNKNOWN CONSEQUENCES

Several days had passed since Jeff and Greg had revealed to their parents the contents of the admission letters.

"Hurry up, Greg. We'll miss the train and then be late for the movie."

"All right, already. I'm moving, I'm moving."

Having time off from their respective kitchens was rare, and getting a chance to hang out together and see a movie, even rarer.

"So your pop looked like he was about to blow a gasket when you read the letter. What happened after we left?" Jeff was curious because he had not got the impression Mr. Anderson was going to deal well with what he had heard.

"For the first ten minutes or so I think he did blow a gasket. I'm pretty sure there were wisps of steam coming from his ears."

Jeff laughed with his friend as they pictured the elder Anderson red faced and shouting. The image was very familiar.

"My mom and pop were pretty cool. Of course, I told them about having applied to the Culinary Institute of America as a back up plan. That seemed to help them get past the bad news. Honestly, they just want me to be happy."

"That's cool." Greg wished his folks could be placated so easily.

"Yeah. I cannot imagine being turned down by the CIA. I just hope what I'll learn there is nearly as good as the French school. So, what's your plan B?"

Greg did not really have a fall back option for not getting into school. Not at first. After the Walkers and Jeff had gone home that afternoon his father had finally got to a point where he could converse intelligibly.

THE PERFECT MEAL

"You are going to that god damned school come hell or high water. I will get up at 4 a.m. and call them tomorrow. You can be sure they are going to get a piece of my mind."

Attempting to be a voice of reason, Greg interjected, "Be careful Father. Yelling and screaming at them might not help my case."

"Gregory is right, dear. The letter did say he would be placed on some sort of waiting list. Surely there will be some applicants who are unable to attend."

"Well I'm not about to leave our son's future to chance. That school is going to hear from me just the same."

Still pink from his tirade, Gerald left his wife and son to attend restaurant business.

Betty commented once Gerald was out of hearing range. "I wouldn't want to cross paths with your father right now if I were one of the employees. Are you doing alright, honey? This must be quite a disappointment for you."

"Not so much. I thought it would be cool to go to France, see the sights and get some good food education. But something has occurred to me that could be just as good."

"What might that be?"

"I'm thinking I might just go to Europe anyway. You and Father were already planning for me to be away, and we can afford it. So why not go and experience some time in the Old World?"

Betty hesitated in responding. "School is one thing dear, but going to just backpack and play? How do you think your father is going to respond to that request?"

The truth was even though her son had completely rejected her affections over the past few years, she still felt close to him. The last thing she wanted was for him to go away.

Greg had never contemplated using their past before. The chance of him getting away from her, from his family life was diminishing with every moment. He made the decision.

"It would really mean a lot to me, Mother, if you would talk to Father on my behalf. Tell him you think it would be a good idea for me to get away. You do want me to be happy, don't you? Tell him I'll even visit some of his suppliers over there. Or if you think it would appease him, have him set up some intern work at his contact's restaurants."

For the first time in years he reached for his mother's hands, squeezing just past the point of her discomfort. Staring directly into her eyes, his tone was even, forceful.

"You will help me, won't you Mother? We don't want our past to become our present. How would Father react to that?"

------ oOo ------

Betty had waited until she and Gerald were preparing for bed to approach the subject of Greg and Europe. It might have been the sense it made for Greg to do restaurant business while there. Or it could have something to do with the fear which motivated her pleading with Gerald. Either way, he finally agreed.

------ oOo ------

The two young men were sprinting up the subway stairs to street level. The movie theater was just half a block away.

"So, your pop agreed to let you just head off to Europe? You have to be kidding me. Wow!"

"I know. Mother really convinced him. But I will have to do some work while I'm over there. Won't be all fun and games."

"Yeah, right. Sure it won't."

The two ducked into the first of the long line of doors in front of the theater. Having purchased tickets and some concessions they proceeded up several floors of escalators in search of their film.

------ oOo ------

Most of Jeff's time had been spent getting mentally ready for the next phase of his life. He was usually in the kitchens early in the morning practicing a technique or studying the effects ingredient substitution had on a dish's final outcome. After working through lunch, doing the prep and finishing dinner service, it would be easy to imagine Jeff falling into deep sleep in preparation to do it all again the next day.

It was common, however, for one of his parents to see the light under his bedroom door at midnight, or later. Usually he was reading cooking theory or food related articles about his favorite celebrity chefs. Noticing her son was still awake as she and Ray were heading to bed, Ruth knocked on Jeff's door.

"Jeffrey, dear. How lucky would you feel if I asked you to be the chef for Lizabeth's upcoming birthday party? As her god parents, your father and I would like to be enjoying the party with her and the Anderson's instead of being hidden away back in the kitchens."

"Hmmm? How lucky would I feel, you ask? How lucky would I feel? Let me ask you this, mother dear. How lucky SHOULD I feel at this amazing opportunity?" There was the slightest tinge of fun sarcasm in his voice.

"Remind me again, dear son, who brought you into this world? Who protected you from the savage elements? Who nourished and made sure you had all your vaccination shots? Who once pushed you out of the way of a speeding train?"

"Uhm, you? Really? A speeding train? Can you remind me again of that horrific experience? I forget the details, mother dear."

His mother could be such a goof ball at times. But he knew she loved him.

"I guess I could do this favor for you, however, I'm pretty sure you'll owe me big time for this one."

There had only been a few times when Jeff had the chance to run the kitchen as head chef. His mother knew there was nothing he wouldn't do to be in charge.

"Well my dear, I am sure you will find some way you mother might be able to repay your doing me this one little favor."

"Big favor."

"Big favor!"

------ oOo ------

Lizbeth's party was in 2 weeks and Jeff should be leaving for school a few weeks after that. Cooking for the party would give him something to focus on other than what his life would be like in a month's time.

The next day Jeff asked Greg to help him out in the kitchen during Lizbeth's party.

"If it will keep me from sitting around watching my parents and your parents and a bunch of snotty kids picking their noses, count me in."

Not the picture Jeff had envisioned for party activities.

"Cool. I appreciate it. And I know I've apologized already, but I am really, really sorry we're not going to school together."

"And like the 40 other times you've told me you're sorry, don't worry about it. That was always my parents dream. Not mine. My biggest challenge is figuring out what country I'm heading off to first. So many choices."

"I'm sure you'll figure out some sort of itinerary. I just feel sorry for the female population of Europe with you on the prowl."

"Whatever, Chef Jeff."

There was something about how Greg pronounced the rhyme. Maybe it had something to do with the fact that Greg also punched him in the arm as he was saying it.

------ oOo ------

The party meal consisted of 4 courses that Jeff would create, and a specially ordered cake his mother had brought in for her god daughter. Between the 3rd and 4th courses, he realized there was not going to be enough plates to finish the service.

"Hey Jonny, could you run some plates through the dishwasher and sanitizer?"

"Sure if you want this final meat course to be super well done shoe leather."

Jeff threw a towel in Jonny's general direction.

"Greg, how about it, man? We're going to need plates to finish up. I think our set up is similar to your dish room."

"You've got it, Chef Jeff," he replied with that rhyme again. Jeff knew he would have to go by Chef Walker at some point in his professional life.

"Thanks, GG," was the first thing Jeff could come up with. Only Greg's little sister had ever called him GG. He still remembered when Greg had turned 13 and unilaterally quashed all use of that nick name. As he was remembering that day, he ducked just in time to miss the sponge hurled from the dish room.

Greg opened the sanitizer after the first load and was struck by the fact there was no rush of steam rolling out under the stainless steel hatch. Sticking his head around the doorway he yelled out.

"Hey Chef Jeff, the sanitizer isn't getting hot."

"Oh yeah. Squeeze back behind the counters and check the gas line sometimes you have to close the valve, open it again and relight the pilot. We've been having problems with it the past few weeks."

Good thing Greg was on the lean side. Not much space to get back to that copper gas line and valve. He could see where the line went through the wall into the cooking area. The valve was very close to the wall and he wondered how it actually opened and closed. It seemed there was not enough room to swing the handle around to shut it off. Reaching for the pipe he noticed some give in the direction of the wall.

"Ah, this must be how they turn the valve."

So he pulled on the pipe just slightly so that there was enough space to actually rotate the valve and shut it off. He waited a few moments, pulled the pipe again and reopened the sanitizer's valve. After the pilot was lit he was back in business.

When Greg pulled the copper line from the wall he was also loosening the T-connector on the other side. It was this connection that fed the gas lines for the 2 stoves, deep fat fryer and salamander which the chefs used to cook their food. The seal was still intact so no gas was leaking. Yet.

8 DESTRUCTION OF A DREAM

Lizbeth's party had been a success and like clockwork, the very next morning, Jeff was down in his family's kitchens working on his craft. As he moved his dish's ingredients over to the stove, he noticed the pan was not nearly as hot as he would have liked.

Leaning over to observe the flame, he was confused to find it only on a medium low height. He turned the knob for that burner down and then back up to high, but the flame never seemed to grow. Changing burners, he found another that seemed to be working fine and shifted his pan to heat up there.

"Mental note, clean out the burner apparatus. Seems they are getting clogged up."

He finished up his breakfast dish and proceeded out of the kitchen until it was time to prep for the lunch service.

Not long thereafter, Ray came down to start the lunch specials a bit early. Today he had decided they would offer a slow roast and wanted to heat the ovens in preparation for the meat. After turning them on, Ray placed a large, oven-proof pot on the stove top with the intentions of getting a nice quick sear on the roast before covering it and placing it on the rack.

Like Jeff had discovered earlier, the flame on that one burner was not nearly high enough to heat the pot adequately. Since there was plenty of time, Ray decided to look into it. Now, all of the burners were acting up. While not in pristine condition, they appeared to be unblocked.

"I wonder what the heck is going on today," Ray muttered to himself. He turned off the burners and made his way to the gas shut off valve. Like the line that fed the sanitizer on the other side of the wall, the kitchen side valve also had to be slightly pulled away from the wall in order to actuate. He closed it, and then reopened the valve. There had been times in the past when the supply sometimes slowed, for whatever reason. Closing and reopening the valves always seemed to do the trick.

Back at the stove, he turned the burner knob. The strong hiss of gas could be heard coming out so Ray was confident the challenge had been corrected. The natural gas he had allowed to escape from the burner prior to lighting the pilot was enough odor to cover the fact that when the master valve had been reopened, the movement of the pipe pushed the stove feed's connection apart far enough for a major flow of gas to start leaking.

The stove had been a part of the restaurant purchase made so many years ago. It was a solid appliance that worked great as long as it was regularly cleaned and degreased. One of the challenges of using an oven and stove top this old was the manual pilot lighting required for operations.

Remembering he needed the oven for his lunch special, Ray opened the door, lit a long wooden match and proceeded to reach his arm, head and half his torso into the commercial oven. It must have been the fact that the oven was shielded from the leaking behind the stove which prevented Ray from being overwhelmed by the gas odor. Whatever kept him from realizing the gas line had separated was unfortunate.

As the flame from the match took to the pilot apparatus the fire was pulled back behind the oven causing ignition and a massive explosion. Ray had no time to extricate himself from the oven before he was engulfed in a fire ball.

Most of his body was instantly set ablaze. Fortunately he entered unconsciousness immediately. Just as fortunately, one of the dishwashers had been setting up in the back, heard the explosion and rushed into the kitchen.

The employee was able to pull Ray away from the stoves and using his apron, started putting out the flames which were consuming his boss. Hearing the explosion, Jeff and his mother quickly made their way down from the living quarters above the restaurant. Both were horrified by what they found in the kitchen.

"Call 911, Mother Hurry," Jeff shouted at his mother as they passed through the dining room's swinging doors. Ruth was aghast and could barely stand to make the call from the kitchen phone just on the wall past the doors.

"What happened? What the hell happened?" He was yelling at the dishwasher.

Not waiting for an answer, Jeff's focus turned to the fire burning along the back wall behind the fryer and stove. He directed the employee to get the fire extinguisher from the back room.

"I'll get the kitchen extinguisher. We have to put out this fire. Now!"

For whatever reason the overhead system had not kicked on to stop the flames. Fortunately for the rest of the kitchen and restaurant, their fast actions prevented complete catastrophe. Unfortunately, the damage which had occurred was still extensive. Not to mention the state of his father.

By the time Jeff had the fire under control, the paramedics were making their way in to help Ray. They had entered the kitchens from the back alley entrance where it was easier and faster to bring their emergency response vehicles. Following closely behind the EMT's were several FDNY with gear, helmets and masks yet to be donned. The firefighters job would be an easy one, and they stood aside so Ray could receive emergency medical treatment.

With nothing left for Jeff to do, he made his way over to his mother. She was now slumped at the chair and desk located near the kitchen entrance. Sobbing while she stared at her husband, she reached out for Jeff as he approached her.

"It's okay, Mother. They are doing everything they can for Pop. They're going to take care of him. Don't worry, don't worry."

But of course she was going to worry. After 29 years of marriage she loved Raymond Walker more than ever. He was her soul mate and to see him lying there unconscious, with most of his body charred, still smoldering, was just about the worst thing she could imagine.

Jeff's parents were never really the type to fight and argue. They had healthy disagreements over the course of his life, but they always seemed to be carried out more on an intellectual basis than an emotional one. Anger and sadness were emotions he had had little exposure to growing up.

The only time he could recall his mother crying profusely was during the celebration of she and his father's 25th wedding anniversary.

Ray had replaced her original wedding ring with one adorned of diamonds and other colorful precious gems. To Ruth, next to her husband and son, it was just about the most beautiful thing she had ever seen.

The EMT's were now in the process of taking Ray out of the kitchen. They had to move slowly as the long stretcher could not navigate around the cook stations and appliances very well.

Ruth was in no condition to drive a vehicle and follow them to the hospital. She would have to wait for Jeff to finish speaking with the fire inspector. Since there was not really much to share, the family was able to follow within a few moments after the ambulance, leaving the inspectors to make their reports.

------ oOo ------

The adrenaline levels in his body only started returning to normal after Jeff and his mother had been sitting in the waiting room for some time. This was one of the hardest things to do. Just sit, wait, and ponder how his father was going to be.

"Going for some more coffee. Can I get you something, Mother?"

"No, honey, I'm fine."

"At least let me get you a sandwich or something. You've not eaten all day, Mother. You need some food to stay energized while we wait."

"I'll have something if you have something."

Jeff let go of his mother's hands and was just turning to leave the room when one of the trauma doctors came through the doors marked "Staff Only". Stopping in his tracks he helped his mother up, placed one arm around her waist and held her clenched hands with his other.

They both watched for the classic signs on the doctor's face as he approached them. If one had to guess, it certainly did not look like he was there to present them with good news.

9 REALITY SETS IN

A few days had passed since the tragedy. Because of the extensive damage caused by the fire there were no meals being made at the Walker's restaurant, no employees, no activity for the most part. Ray had been removed from intensive care but was still in near critical condition.

The doctors had informed Jeff and his mother that while most of Ray's body had received extensive burns he would likely live through the ordeal. This was the good news. The bad was that in addition to massive scarring and the need for a number of surgeries, the chance of Ray ever being able to stand for long periods of time or have effective dexterity with his hands and fingers was minimal. Raymond Walker had been forced into an early retirement.

He was just beginning to find his voice again and the hoarse, scratchy sounds he was making startled Ruth awake. She had been by his side nearly every moment since they had brought him out of the operating room. It was now late enough to be dark outside, but still within visiting hours. Jeff had left his parents for the evening. Ruth had slipped into one of those moments when it was hard to determine whether one was truly asleep, awake or lost somewhere in between.

"Ruth. Dear Ruth. What happened?" Those few words were long and laborious coming from the smoke damaged mouth and throat of her husband. Reaching for his cup of water she bent the straw allowing him to sip and wet his throat.

"Oh, Ray. Ray. There was some sort of accident while you were lighting the stove's pilot. Apparently the gas lines feeding the appliances had worked loose and a leak started just before you were in the oven lighting it. We should have replaced those appliances long ago. How are you feeling, honey? Should I get the doctor?"

It was as difficult to clear his thoughts as it was to clear his throat. "Restaurant?" he whispered.

Ruth paused, gulping before she attempted to explain to him.

"There was a lot of damage, honey. Pretty much every thing along the fire wall connected to the gas line was damaged beyond repair. The inspectors were unable to find any reasons for the overhead extinguishers not to work, but they didn't and that caused even more damage. If Jeff hadn't gotten there with the kitchen's portable extinguisher we might have lost so much more. But none of that matters right now dear. All that matters is you getting better."

She leaned in to kiss him, but knew the bandages on his face would not permit her embrace to be felt. She just moved close so he would have no trouble seeing the love in her eyes.

"I love you, more than anything, Raymond Walker. Don't you stop fighting. Don't you dare."

------ oOo ------

With so much to do in the aftermath of the fire, and his mother spending nearly all of her time at the hospital, Jeff was left trying to get the family business back on its feet. This morning he had to deal with the insurance company representative and get everything squared away so they could get their claim check and start ordering new kitchen appliances.

How was he going to get everything back in order before he left for school? As he pondered the growing number of tasks he heard the front doors open and went out to greet the insurance rep.

"Hello. Are you," the man paused to consult the papers in his file, "Jeffrey Walker?"

"Hi. That would be me. And I'm betting you are Mr. Jenkins from the insurance company? You can call me Jeff."

He offered the man a seat asking if there was something he might like to drink. Jeff knew that it was wise to make everything go as smoothly as possible.

"Thank you, no," Jenkins refused in a polite, business-like manner. "This really won't take that long. Our investigators have reviewed the official reports filed by both the fire inspector as well as the emergency medical technicians. Based upon the findings and the guidelines our company adheres to in matters like these, we are forced to deny your claims for payment. The requests for equipment replacement value will not be paid, according to the policy coverage."

This was not what he had expected to hear. "Uhm, excuse me. What did you say? Your company is not going to write a check to my parents to help rebuild from this accident? Why on earth not? How can you possibly not cover this. It was clearly an accident."

THE PERFECT MEAL

"I understand your frustration, Mr., er, Jeff. The investigators at our company have determined that the cause of this situation is not a cut and dry case of accident. Based upon the accounts reported by the fire inspector, the gas lines look as if they were worked loose by deliberate measure. None of those appliances caused the explosion on their own. Add to this the fact there was nothing at all wrong with the overhead extinguishing system. Based upon the reports it simply did not come on. It is almost as if someone," the way he said 'someone' irritated Jeff, "turned off the master switch to the fire suppressant system, and then turned it on after the fire had been put out "

"Surely you're kidding, right? Who on earth would do all that just to get a new stove and deep fat fryer? Are you insane? Have you been to see my father? I think he might argue with your theory."

"Ah, yes. As to the disposition of covering Mr. Walker's medical bills. The company has been unable to determine whether his actions constitute malice and forethought as to a desire to defraud his insurers. Again, according to the reports your father was found with his head and upper body inside an oven that had gas leaking. Not to be indelicate, but these are not uncommon findings in many suicide attempts. Attempts, which when fail their prescribed goal are then filed with insurers in hopes of receiving benefits. Again, you have my condolences, Mr. Walker, however our findings are final."

There was little Jeff knew to say in the moments following this mans explanation. His company would not be honoring the claim they had made on a policy which was in good standing and had been for years. Sitting there, slack jawed, he could only watch as Jenkins left the restaurant. After a few moments , he reacted.

"Fuck. Fuck. Fuck. FUCK!"

Greg entered the restaurant and overheard the uncharacteristic expletives being uttered.

"Hey, Jeff. I know what happened to your dad sucks. But come on man, sitting in an empty room cussing at the walls isn't going to make anything better. Can I help?"

"Did you see that guy in the suit who left just before you got here?"

"I think so. I was just waiting for traffic to clear and cross the street as he was getting into his car and driving off. Why?"

Taking a deep breath, Jeff summarized the second explosion to hit his family's restaurant.

"Whoa. What the hell? Are you serious? Say you're just messing around."

"I wish I could. I really wish I could. I have no idea what we are going to do now. Can you imagine how much the hospital bills alone are going to set us back? Not to mention replacing the appliances and getting the kitchen ready to reopen."

"Surely you're folks have money saved up that will help with all these bills, right?"

"They have a little. Maybe enough to cover getting a new stove and stuff. But you know how expensive this medical stuff can be. Man, this really bites."

Greg was doing his best to console his friend, but the situation was looking grim.

"Things are going to work out man. You'll see. Something good usually comes out of the bad things that happen to us. Hang in there."

"I hope you're right. Everything in my entire life just crashed around me."

For the first time since receiving the bad news it occurs to Jeff he has a reasonable amount of money in his education fund.

"I cannot imagine heading away now, leaving Mother to care for Pop and try to get this place back in shape. You know what this means?" He doesn't wait for a reply. "It means I'm going to have to cough up the money I was going to use for school over the next 2 years and help pay my pop's medical bills and get this place going again. It's the only way."

Greg is immediately struck by the gravity of what this will mean to his best friend. Jeff leaves to go to the hospital and tell his folks about the insurance and the fact that he is no longer heading off to any culinary school, anywhere.

10 ENTER ANGELA

Ruth forbade Jeff from telling Raymond what he was planning to do. She knew, deep inside there was no other way until they had a chance to fight the insurance company. But then, their attorney indicated a legal battle might take much longer and cost far more money to win than they were willing to spend.

According to the doctors, Jeff's father was recovering in good fashion. He spent as much time with his dad as possible, giving his mother some time to go home and refresh herself. She hated being away from Ray, even for those few moments but definitely needed time to process everything happening to their family. Especially the sacrifices her son was making for their welfare.

"Hey, Pop. Man, you're looking sharper every day. Trust you're going to get out of this bed soon and get back to bossing me around the kitchens?" Jeff knew his father would never again be able to work the kitchens or boss anyone around for that matter. It was going to be a long time before he would even be able to get out of a bed and go to the bathroom by himself.

"All those years of growing new arms and legs, how come we never practiced developing a new covering of skin?" Ray's voice was much less labored. There was just a touch of a smile in there somewhere as well. "Don't you worry kiddo, you'll be handling things from now on. You're an amazing young cook. You'll be fine running that line."

Jeff smiled. He so wanted to let his father know he decided not to go to school, but his mother had yet to share the insurance company news with him. It was important to keep spirits up and be as positive as possible.

Still, now that Ray was recuperating and had been moved out of the critical ward, his faculties were back and his sense of time and dates prompted his query.

"Hey Jeff, I know your mother has been withholding certain things from me. She probably is worried about my general frame of mind. So, I'm going to stick it to you and force you to fill me in. If I'm not mistaken, weren't you supposed to have left for school two or three days…"

"Come on, Pop," Jeff cut him off. "Cool it. You know that Mom will kick my butt if you make me spill the beans."

"You might think I'm not able to kick your butt right now, but that doesn't mean I won't remember to do it later when I am fit as a fiddle. So, commence to bean spilling, kiddo."

Jeff appreciated the fact that his father had the fortitude to crack jokes, so he shared the bad news about no insurance money, and canceling his acceptance to the CIA. This time he was responsible for raiding his school fund to help pay bills and buy new appliances.

"Aw, kid. If I'd have been one quarter the man you are when I was your age, well, I'd have been one quarter of a man." It was the wink in Ray's eye that told Jeff the depth of his father's appreciation. That was all he needed.

"Just get better, Pop. Mom and I need you healthy. She needs you more than anything. There are plenty of good local cooking schools where I can learn. Once our place is back up and running, I'll have a real world laboratory to apply everything they teach me. You know I love you and mom, our family, more than anything else. Period. I'm not worried or upset. Just get better. Okay?"

------ oOo ------

Angela Harris had cared for her father for several years. Between the Social Security payments he had received and her part time work, they were able to get by financially, but there was very little extra. Over the past few months since he had been buried, she was unsure what to do with herself or the general direction her life would take.

At only 20 years old, Angela was smart and had a well developed common sense. Physically, she was in extremely good shape, the result of long distance running. People from outside of New York might not realize the runner's mecca the City was. Angela had been and continued to be quite the athlete. What few friends she had time for were all runners as well.

Between looking after her ailing father and the job, she dated very little. The reality was date requests rarely came her way. One could hardly label the cat calls, hoots and hollers of construction workers during her early morning runs romantic. Besides, most of the boys her age physically, held little attraction for her mentally or emotionally.

When David Harris, her father's younger brother by ten years, called with an opening in his restaurant supply delivery business she jumped at the opportunity. David had always connected with his niece and felt it was his duty to help out since his brother's death.

THE PERFECT MEAL

She had started out in the offices taking calls and arranging the schedule for pick ups and drop offs. But Angela was sharp, energetic and wanted to get out, move around the city for a while. For years, her time was spent waiting on her ailing father, rarely leaving his side. Now she had tasted a bit of life. She wanted a larger bite. David finally gave in and when an opening on one of the delivery trucks was available he put her on it.

The schedule of deliveries that day was about like every other she had experienced for the past several weeks. First thing this morning they would be dropping off a new oven, stove, fryer and various other appliances. No one on her truck ever complained about her share of the work load. Pulling up in the alley behind the restaurant, she jumped out in search of a manager to sign for and receive the goods. Just through the back entrance, she spotted a young man about her age who was chatting with someone in an apron.

"Excuse me, we've got a delivery for you. Can you sign here so we can get this stuff unloaded?" She handed him the clipboard.

Greg was pretty sure they had not ordered any appliances, but this young woman was really cute, so he stalled while trying to chat her up.

"Hmmm," tapping the pen to the clipboard, acting as if he was reviewing the listed items, "I'm Greg, what's your name?"

"Angela Harris, Harris Supplies. Everything look right?"

"Not sure Angela Harris, Harris Supplies. But I would have to say that everything about you looks right. What do you say about going out with me before I head off to France? Just found out I was accepted to cooking school in Paris and will be leaving next week."

It was not that Greg was bad looking but his approach was pushy, completely out of context for someone she met thirty seconds prior. There was also a bit of arrogance about his culinary school boasts.

"Congratulations. You're offer is very thoughtful, however, no. Thank you, but I see no reason to start dating someone who's leaving the country."

"Really? How can you not want to hang out with me? Who's talking about dating? Just dinner, a movie, whatever might come next. Oh, I get it. You must have a boyfriend, right?"

"Will that get you off my back? If I have a boyfriend, will you leave me alone and let me deliver these appliances, Mr. Walker?"

"Oh, you must have the new kitchen appliances for the restaurant that caught fire across the street. I'm Greg Anderson. We get mail and stuff for them all the time. In fact, poor Chef Jeff was supposed to be heading off to school with me, but can't now that he has to take over running his family's business. So, what do you say, Gorgeous? Change your mind? You'll have a great time. Guaranteed!"

Realizing her truck was at the wrong address, she snatched the clipboard from Greg and headed outside. He was not gross to her, but she had no

inclination to casually date someone who was likely to be gone for a number of years. Better to just focus on her work, and leave the complications to get on
planes to France.

"Have a great time at school. We're on a tight schedule today. Be seeing you."

She could not have gotten away faster. Boys could be real pains to her at times. Most of the time, actually. She directed the truck's driver to head over to the alley behind the restaurant across the street.

Arriving at the back of Walker's she was met by Ruth. While happy at the prospect her kitchen would be operational again soon, there was still an overriding sadness at all which had occurred to the family recently. Angela approached Ruth and inquired of the address and name on the account.

"For some reason we had your address confused with the restaurant across the street. I had the lovely misfortune of meeting a Greg Anderson over there."

It must have been that she was talking to a sweet looking, older woman which allowed Angela to open and share how she felt about the unwanted advance.

Noticing the shudder in Angela's expression, Ruth smiled as she replied, "Gregory is okay. He can be a little arrogant and pushy at times, but he's not to be worried about."

"If you say so, Mrs. Walker. But the way he tried to impress me with his talk of going to France for cooking school was a little more arrogance than I personally like in a man."

Ruth had not been told about Greg getting an acceptance notification to the school in Paris. "Oh," she shared the highlights of all that had happened to Jeff, her husband and the restaurant with Angela. "My son is such a lovely young man, Angela. I'll bet the two of you would make fast friends. And since he won't be going off to school, perhaps you might be interested in meeting? I know I'm partial about Jeff, but I have a good feeling about you as well."

Carrying a tall stack of boxes filled with produce, Jeff blindly walks through the open back door, nearly colliding with Angela and his mother. Just back from a nearby farmers market, most of Jeff's days are filled with thoughts only of the work to be done and getting closer to reopening.

"Pardon me, mother. I didn't see you two standing there."

"Honey, did you notice we were getting the new appliances today? This is Angela Harris. She's here to install the stove and other things."

Always polite, even in his absent mindedness, "Hello Ms. Harris. Please accept my apologies for nearly crushing you with a bunch of produce."

Seeing how handsome he was, a smile crept over her face. It was a look of interest which did not escape Mrs. Walker. Unfortunately, Jeff, caught up in his thoughts, failed to make any significant connection. Being ever resourceful, Ruth stopped her son before he escaped the company of the two women.

"Jeffrey, I think we should invite Angela to our grand reopening. Without her bringing us the new equipment we'd still be waiting to get things going again. What do you say, honey?"

"Sounds lovely to me, Mom. Ms. Harris, would you be so kind as to join us next week when we are back in business? It would be my pleasure to thank you again with a wonderful meal and the company of my mother."

That smile was the brightest thing he had seen on Ruth's face in a long time. That pleased him. Angela's smile also caught his attention and he realized what a lovely woman she was. Now he was actually looking forward to something with some cheer and anticipation.

Expressing her thanks and leaving to finish up the delivery, Angela realized that Mrs. Walker had just set she and her son up, on a sort of date.

"Thank you so much, Mrs. Walker, Jeff. I look forward to next week."

Standing at the other end of the hallway was Greg with some mail for the Walker's. He had watched the entire exchange and was incensed at the fact that it was Jeff who would be spending quality time with this beauty he had met first. Leaving before anyone noticed him, he tossed the envelopes on a table and went back to his place across the street.

As Jeff was unloading the produce from the boxes, his mother felt the need to share what she had learned about Greg and culinary school.

"I'm sure he's meant to tell you, Jeff, honey. I am so sorry you had to learn about it this way. Please don't let it affect your friendship with him."

But it was too late for that. Jeff thought they had been friends. Originally they were going to spend that time in France hanging out together and learning everything about food and cooking. Now it was Greg Anderson who was going to be living his dream.

"Wow! Not even the decency to tell me himself, but instead trying to brag to women about his accomplishments."

He could only walk away from the task at hand, as well as his mother. From the way Ruth looked at him, he knew her sadness was returning. He kissed her and went to carry out other duties, promising to find a way to overcome these feelings.

11 PEN PALS

Betty was certain she would be in for much more of a fight about Gerald going to visit the ailing Raymond Walker.

"Are you okay Gerry?"

"Of course, Bet. Why?"

"I just asked you to go and visit your self-proclaimed arch nemesis as he recovers in the hospital. And all you could say to me was yes?"

Gerald had actually been considering he should make the pilgrimage for several days now. Since his son had been accepted to the school in France there had been a cloak of guilt upon his shoulders. Not something he enjoyed wearing.

"Ah, sweet Bet. I've truly been an ass towards Ray all these years, haven't I?"

Betty had never seen such contrition in her husband.

"You're slipping whiskey into your morning coffee, aren't you, dear?" Secretly, she was hoping that now was the time she and Ruth had always hoped would someday arrive.

"No. No whiskey, though I may need some after I come from visiting him. Hell, he may suffer a heart attack when he sees me enter his hospital room. Are we sure I should be doing this?"

"You get out of here right now and go express your well wishes to that man. I know for a fact he would appreciate seeing you. Go. Now, Gerald Anderson!"

Prior to leaving New York, Greg had looked up the mailing address of the Harris Supply Company. He wanted to be able to send letters to Angela. Even though she clearly did not fancy his attention, he still thought she was sweet, pretty and with a feisty attitude that if nothing else would make for a nice

friendship.

Staring out his window on the Air France flight, Greg was still actively contemplating the past few days. Since he had seen Angela Harris at the Walker's, Jeff had been very cold towards him.

Before landing in Paris, he started writing her the first of many letters to come over the next couple of years. In this one, he had better send a convincing apology and let her know how much he regretted coming on in such an arrogant, thoughtless manner.

She may never end up being his girlfriend, but that did not excuse him from not attempting to right the wrong he had committed. Besides, even if she and Jeff hit it off, at least she would be around when he got back from school. At worst, the

three of them would have fun and enjoy hanging out together. This, of course, assuming that Jeff Walker was going to find a way to forgive him for having absconded with his long held dreams, goals and desires. Maybe he should start writing Jeff as well. Greg would have to ponder that a while longer.

"I probably should have told him sooner about the school," Greg thought to himself. "But how could I possibly lay waste to my friend's dreams and desires? Of course, he's treated me like I don't really exist since he did find out. I wonder if he knew I made a move on Angela? Whatever the case, I have to go and make my parents proud."

There was nothing but clouds and the deep, blue Atlantic Ocean out the window. It was going to be a long flight and Greg was tired. Tipping his hat forward over his eyes, he pushed his seat back and drifted to sleep.

------ oOo ------

Ray had not suffered a heart attack when Gerald arrived at his hospital room. Surprised? Yes.

"I'll be honest, Gerald. I would have lost the bet if someone had told me you'd be one of my visitors. I have enjoyed seeing Betty when she's accompanied my Ruth on occasion. Thank you for coming."

"No need to thank me, Ray. I should have been here sooner, but I just didn't know how you might take the fact that Jeff was forced to stay home, Greg going to France instead."

At first Ray had been extremely frustrated with all that had transpired. "Things happen, and we either accept them or allow them to eat at us. I admit I was unhappy for my son. But never have I held ill feelings towards Gregory, or the rest of your family, Gerald. Your boy is a talented young cook in his own right. He very much deserves to get this opportunity."

Realizing he could learn some humility from Ray, Gerald asked what he could do to help the Walker's out.

"Anything you need, Ray. Just ask. Betty and I very much want to see you back on your feet as soon as possible."

"You and me both. They tell me I'm to be released next week, but there are number of surgeries I'll have to go through over the next year or so. It's that damned insurance company that is causing us the problems now. The money from Jeff's education fund will only go so far towards rebuilding our kitchen. With the medical bills piling up, we're not sure how things are going to play out. But we'll figure things out. Thanks for your offer."

Gerald thought he saw a way to extend his new friend some help. "Why don't you and Ruth allow Betty and I help you out with the finances. We have some money from one of Bet's relatives who died last year."

"I couldn't possibly ask you to give us money, Gerald."

"Look, you need the money, so let's call it a loan. Our familys have known each other long enough, I don't think you'll skip out. If you were to get a loan from the bank, you'd have to pay them, right? I'll have a legitimate contract drawn up, and as collateral you can put up, oh, I know. You can put up Jeff. What do you say?"

Ray strained to recall if he had ever heard Gerald make any sort of joke before.

"Well, since you put it that way, I guess you might have a valid point. But I could only agree to half of my only son as collateral for the loan. Two thirds at most."

"Deal, Ray. You drive a hard bargain."

Their handshake was not as hearty as it might have been, for Ray's hands were still covered in bandages. The two men sat and talked a couple hours more. Perhaps they were mellowing out in their old age.

Later, after Ruth found out about her husband's acceptance of Gerald's offer, she immediately called Betty. The women were giggling on the phone like school girls. Finally, after all these years and after such a tragedy, their husbands seemed to embrace a friendship of their own.

"Can you believe it, Betty? Not only am I impressed that you got Gerald to go see Ray, but the fact he offered him a loan to help with our expenses? What did you do to that husband of yours, honey?"

"You're so silly Ruth. I just pointed out that if he didn't go and be cordial I might be withholding certain favors for the rest of his natural life. Well, maybe not that long, but I didn't tell him that."

There was a cheeriness in Betty's voice. She shared that her uncle had passed away last year. There was a substantial amount of money he had left her, and it was just sitting in a CD in the bank.

THE PERFECT MEAL

"With the savings rates as low as they are, it was rather easy for me to convince my businessman husband that you all could pay the same amount in interest and he wouldn't lose a penny of money on the investment."

"As always, you are the very best friend I could ever imagine having in my life, Betty Anderson. I'll never be able to thank you enough for helping us. We are going to use a bit of the loan to convert the flats upstairs into individual units and look to generate some rental income from them. That should help us even more with repaying you."

"Honestly, Ruth. I don't personally care if we ever see that money again, but I know your Raymond won't allow a debt to go unpaid. Especially to my Gerry. But I have to say, I really think those two are beginning to hit it off famously. That's worth more to me than a few dollars sitting around in a bank account."

"You're sweet. So we'll see you two, tomorrow evening at our reopening party, right? We are so excited!"

"We wouldn't miss it for the world. I only wish Greg could be here as well. I think he and Jeff have drifted apart with all that's happened."

"They'll work things out, Betty. Don't worry, I'm sure they will."

12 TEMPERATURE RISING

Eight months had passed since Jeff and his mother successfully reopened their family restaurant. Much had changed, though not all of it good. The money which the Andersons had lent his family saved their lives. As much as Jeff hated being in debt to Mr. Anderson, and by extension, to Greg, there had really been no other options.

Ray had finally been released and after 2 surgeries, seemed to at least have leveled off with regards to his ability to start taking care of himself. Moving around was a slow, challenging process and at times he would get down on himself about not recovering faster.

It was easy for Ray to intellectually do fine, but with the levels of pain he still had to endure, his patience was on a far shorter fuse than in the past. The one thing he had begun to enjoy was when Gerald would come and offer to take him out to a park and get some fresh air.

"What's the latest from that son of yours, Gerry? Has he mastered the souffle yet? Jeff still has challenges doing that."

"From his last letter home, I believe he's doing extremely well with learning the various cooking techniques. But I'm really excited about what seems to be his growing passion for cooking in general. Both his mother and I are very pleased to be reading how interested he is in all things food related."

"Splendid. I know exactly how you feel. I'm still impressed that Jeffrey gets up every morning to practice something new he's read about or learned in one of the extension courses he's been taking the past several months."

"You've quite a fine kid there, Walker. I should have held strong for the whole kit and caboodle as collateral on that loan of yours."

THE PERFECT MEAL

"Speaking of which, they finished installing the elevator in that space which will be at the back of the building and the end of the hallway. I cannot tell you how much that has helped me get in and out of the place. Now if they'll just finish up the banging and clanging with the upper flats, I might actually get a decent night of rest."

Gerald was thankful his building had already been converted prior to his purchase of it. Sleep was far too important to him at this point in his life.

"I hear you, Ray. Really, I do. We'd best be heading back. Looks like some rain coming in and I do not want your wife coming after me if you experience even a single raindrop. I'm sure she'll accuse me of trying to cause you pneumonia. Women."

The two men shared a hearty laugh as Gerald proceeded to push the wheelchair which was allowing Ray to get back out and into the world. Hopefully within the next few months his therapy would allow him to dispense with the contraption and walk completely on his own again. Ray's internal dialogue was constantly reinforcing the fact he was depending upon others more than he cared for.

"I may never get back into that kitchen, but I will get out of this damned chair. I'm glad to have a good friend like Gerry, but am sick and tired of him pushing me around. He did that for years before the accident. The sooner he stops the better I'll feel about so many things including our new friendship."

The two men glided into the back entrance of Walker's restaurant seconds before the heavy rains started falling.

With a bundle of mail and tugging an umbrella against the sudden wind, Betty popped into the front entrance of Walker's just after the rains started. As she entered, Ruth was passing from the dining room into the kitchen. She followed her friend and both caught sight of their husbands chuckling about something. Likely nefarious.

Ruth spoke up first. "And just what do we have here? I know you two were not out in that rain storm. Right?"

More laughter from the men. In their minds the predictable behavior of their wives was too much fun to pass up.

"Nope," exclaimed Ray, "Gerry here had this contraption rolling at, what Gerry, about 35 miles per hour?"

"At least. No way I was getting yelled at for causing your husband to get a cold. Or a chill. Or an unscheduled bath."

Before Ruth could reach the men, Betty landed a solid whack on her husband's back side with the stack of mail she had brought over to her friend.

"Thank you, Betty. You've saved me the trouble."

"Oh, feel free to help yourself in the future. Any time you find it necessary."

The men decided they could not get out of the kitchen fast enough and bee lined it to the new elevator.

"Men. Can't live with them acting as mortal enemies, really can't live with them as best friends," Ruth's insight elicited a quick giggle from Betty.

Ruth flipped through the envelopes Betty had brought over and noticed one addressed to Angela. It appeared to be airmail from France. There was only one person she knew there, Gregory Anderson. As much as she loved the Andersons for all they had done to help her family, she only hoped that Greg was not attempting to come between her Jeffrey and his new girlfriend.

From her perspective, the relationship between her son and Angela Harris had blossomed beautifully. Ruth had known instinctively when she orchestrated their getting together on that fateful appliance installation day that she had done the right thing.

Angela was one of the sweetest young women she had ever met. After Jeff had been dating her for a few months, she was not surprised when he came and asked her permission to have Angela move into one of the available flats with him. Ruth loved having this thoughtful, intelligent and caring young woman nearby, and figured having her move in would strengthen the emotional bonds with Jeff.

Ironically, it was Raymond who had initially objected to the girl moving in.

"Ruth, he is focused on becoming a great chef. They aren't even married yet. Why are you pushing the two of them to live in sin?"

Hearing her husband try and use mortal sin as an excuse for keeping his son away from the woman he loved made Ruth laugh. Loud.

"Uhm, excuse me, Mr. Walker, but how many months did you make excuses to a certain Mr. Myers, about why you were unable to make an honest woman of his daughter? 6? 8? It's been so many years ago, I really cannot remember. Hmmm. I wonder how those months of living in sin turned out?"

Ray hated when she was right, but when she was, and that was most of the time, she was right. He actually liked Angela nearly as much as his wife did. He only hoped she would not prevent his son from reaching his full potential in the kitchen. Jeff had already hurdled much more than his fair share.

Not wanting to bring the letter to Betty's attention, Ruth simply cycled it through and placed the stack on the nearby desk. Angela would be in soon and would retrieve it then.

------ oOo ------

The letter Greg mailed last week must have been the tenth or twelfth he had sent home to Angela. In all that time, she had never replied, but thanks to his mother, he knew Angela was getting them. Betty had informed her son that his two friends had recently moved in together. Since Greg was very familiar with that address, he had started sending his friend her messages there.

On break from classes for a few days, Greg and his roommate were walking around Paris doing some exploring of sights and ducking into little shops here and there.

"Maybe I should just stop mailing them to her," Greg lamented to his friend. "I'm not being obscene with what I say to her. Just doing my best to be a friend. Share a bit about everything we're doing over here. Is that so crazy?"

"You're more persistent a man, than I am, Greg. No, I don't think that's crazy. Maybe you should send her a little token gift of friendship. That might do the trick, no?"

Turning a corner, the two were confronted with an antique curio shop. Taking it as a sign, Greg suggested they go in.

"Perhaps I'll find something interesting here that will make Angela believe I'm an okay guy."

He was speaking more to himself than anyone else. As he looked around the shop, he found all sorts of fascinating items, but none that really seemed to capture the spirit of what he was hoping to express. Having made a complete journey around the inside of the store, Greg decided their finding this place might not have been a sign after all. With his hand on the doorknob and his roommate halfway out, a voice called to them from the back of the shop.

"I may have what you seek, young man. Come here, come here."

Greg was unable to see exactly where the voice was coming from, but figured they were there, what could it hurt to go back and see his offerings. As they retraced their steps towards the rear counters he eventually saw a short, weathered looking fellow. The old man was smiling like he possessed a secret.

"You are in love, yes? You wish to impress your female friend with something to express that love, yes? You wish to ignite the magic between you and she, yes?"

Yes! With all his heart he wanted to scream yes, but his brain told him to respond otherwise.

"No, no sir. I have a lovely friend at home and I want to send her a simple token to express that I miss her and hope our friendship will continue to grow stronger. In fact, it should not be romantic in the least bit, sir."

The shopkeeper had an item in mind, but he proceeded to root around in the boxes behind the counter where he stood. Occasionally he would start to pull something out, look up towards Greg, then, muttering to himself in French, he would replace the item. This went on for several minutes and finally, losing patience, Greg thanked the man and turned to leave.

"Wait, wait, wait. Here it is. I've found you the perfect gift of friendship. It will provide you with the exact temperature of the relationship between you and your female acquaintance."

Curious, Greg returned to the counter to discover just what this bizarre, little man might have found for him. Waiting for his eyes to focus on the box, the proprietor slowly opened it. Perhaps with more flourish than necessary.

"But it's a meat thermometer. Are you serious? A MEAT THERMOMETER?"

"Ah, very observant young man. What else do you see?" the old man asked as he lifted the temperature gauge out of its satin lined resting place. He handed it to Greg for closer inspection.

"It seems to be made of brass, maybe copper, which is a little unusual. It's quite heavy, and it looks old. Must be some sort of antique."

"Anything else?" the shopkeeper urged Greg further.

"What is that on the dial? Some sort of precious gem? That's actually kind of cool. Cannot say I've ever seen a meat thermometer quite so fancy. Does it work?"

"But of course, young man, of course. But there is more."

Try as he might, Greg was unable to note anything further about the kitchen tool. Holding it out for his roommate to inspect, they finally acquiesced.

"It is not what you can see, but what you cannot. This fine instrument was actually made in your great country sometime after the turn of the century. Before one of our greatest chefs had proven himself to the world, he had fallen into a love that was never meant to be. Her father forbid the marriage of his daughter to a young, and at the time, unproven kitchen worker. Though her love for him was true, it was not deeper than the honor she felt at obeying her father."

As the shopkeeper spoke, Greg continued to stare at the thermometer. He noticed how much the stone in the dial was catching the low light in the room and sparkling.

"With much regrets, the lovely woman could only offer her true love a gift of friendship as they were forced apart. Forever. The chef had a long, successful career. He had used her gift every single day, and never in all that time had forgotten her. It is said that on his very deathbed he vowed upon this very instrument that some day the holder of this lowly meat thermometer would be able to experience both a passion for creating the perfect meal as well as loving the perfect mate."

Greg found himself laughing, "So a magic meat thermometer, eh? You're trying to sell me a magic meat thermometer with a shiny stone on it?"

If nothing else, he thought the story would be worth the purchase price for the fun he would have retelling it.

"Ah, not a true believer," the shopkeeper observed. "Perhaps this is not the gift for you after all. Pardon me. There may be something else of interest which you can believe in."

Taking the thermometer from Greg's hand, the old man replaced it in the wooden box and started to move it from the counter top. Reaching over and grabbing the man's arm, Greg stopped him from returning it to storage. In the dim light, Greg missed the smile which appeared momentarily on the old man's face.

"Wait, wait. The story you tell is actually quite enticing. And while I don't fancy Angela and I will ever be more than friends, I think she would be able to accept this as a true token of my friendship for her. I'll take it, sir. I'll take it."

Setting the box down again, the man turned for some heavy, brown wrapping paper. "As you wish young man. As you wish."

13 RE-GIFTING

Jeff was actually quite surprised that his parents had given in so easily, allowing Angela to move in with him to the first finished apartment above their family flat. He had figured his mother would put up the most resistance, but was quite shocked to hear from her that his father had raised certain concerns.

"Pop really used the phrase 'living in sin'?"

"He really did, Jeffrey. But you must understand that as we get older, one of the first things that goes is our ability to remember certain aspects of our past. Especially the things which conflict with how we are living today."

"Ahhhh. That explains so much about why you and Pop act the way you act. Duly noted," he winked and started to laugh.

"Shhh. Don't tell anyone, young man. You know I brought you into this world, I can, well, not really sure what I could do now, you much bigger and stronger than I am. Don't forget to respect your elders. You'll be one before you know it."

"Not on you life, lady."

"How are things going now that Angela has settled in with you upstairs?"

"Pretty well, but still adjusting. I've never really had my own space, and as soon as I'm bestowed the luxury of an apartment, I go and populate it with someone else. But I'm certainly not complaining. We're getting there."

"That's good to hear. It was during that living in sin phase your father and I worked out all our kinks."

"Mom, you and Pop's sexual proclivities are your own business. You really don't need to share your kink tales with me."

THE PERFECT MEAL

Ruth simply could not hold back and smacked her grown little boy on the rump. "That should teach you, young man." They both chuckled at that one.

"Not sure if you've noticed, Mom, but Angela seems to get a letter every few weeks from Greg. I've not really asked her about it. And she's not really said anything about it, either. Should I be concerned?"

This was exactly what Ruth was hoping was not going to happen within that triangle of friends. "I'm sure if you had something to worry about, you would feel it, dear. Do you really think Angela would have moved in with you if she was harboring secret feelings for Gregory Anderson?"

"No, probably not. I guess I'm worrying about nothing then."

"You just focus on continuing to develop your relationship with her, and focus on your food. One is very blessed to know what they truly should be pursuing in life, and you seem to have your sights fixed solidly. Don't allow things yet to happen to create unnecessary havoc and turmoil for you."

"Ah, there's the mother I know and love. Seriously though, thanks for the insight. I'm so fortunate to have a mother that still remembers, at least some of the things she learned earlier in her life."

That comment elicited another big boy spanking.

------ oOo ------

Angela was riding the subway home from the supply offices. In her lap she held a small box which Greg had sent her from France. Though she had yet to reply to one of his letters, there was really no reason she could think of for not being polite and responding to him as a friend. She was sitting next to the her company's office receptionist, and decided to confide in her.

"And so, he's sent me about a dozen letters, and now this. A meat thermometer. A lovely, antique meat thermometer, but what should I make of it, Shelly?"

"Well, I'd love to have 2 boys interested in me. Hell, girl, I'd love for just one to even know that I'm alive."

"Shelly, what are you talking about? Guys give you the eye all the time. What about Joseph on truck 2? Did you not have a date with him a while back?"

"Uhm, if you call a discount movie and hot dogs at the stand outside the theater a date, then, uhm, yeah."

"Oh, poor Shelly. I didn't realize it was such a lovely affair. You have my condolences."

"But regarding your issues, boss lady. If this Greg fellow has done nothing but show you friendship ever since his pig-like come on to you, maybe he deserves a break?"

"Maybe," Angela pondered the concept a moment. "Maybe you're right. I am living with Jeff now, and while I think he spends a little to much time obsessing with food and the restaurant, who am I to judge someone with so much dedication?"

"Yeah, who are you to judge? Besides, nothing lasts forever. Not saying you and the food fanatic aren't going to be together forever, and have little foodies running around some day, but…"

"Little foodies. That's a cute one, Shelly."

"Hey if Greg is being honest with you and simply wants to repent for being a dick, what can it hurt for you to accept him as a friend? We can always use another true friend. Of course, the moment he comes on to you, kick his ass to the curb. Or better yet, send him my way."

That got a big smile from Angela. "Silly. I'll send him your way as soon as he returns from France, if you like. We're just friends. REMEMBER?"

Angela's stop was next. She got up from her seat next to Shelly in preparation to leave. As she moved towards the doors, she asked a young man, standing nearby if he would like to sit next to her lovely friend. Unfortunately for Shelly, the person Angela had so nicely offered her seat to was just this side of hideous looking. Shelly took the opportunity while the man was sitting down to stick out a tongue at her departing boss.

Still several blocks from reaching her new apartment above the Walker's restaurant, Angela figured it was probably time to share with Jeff the letters she had been receiving the past few months. She would even offer to show them to him, should he not believe her about their content.

One of the nice things about living above the place where one worked was the commute to and from the job. Jeff very much enjoyed just having to run up the stairs and take the elevator back down when he needed a quick break from meal prep. With nearly 2 hours until the dinner service started, he completely allowed himself to be enticed by Angela's advances when she came through the kitchen en route to their apartment.

"Seems things are in control down here, Chef Walker. What do you say you meet me upstairs in 10 minutes? I might have something for you when you arrive."

"Is it bigger than a bread box, Ms. Harris?"

"Well that depends upon what boundaries you decide to lay out. It could be much, much bigger, or perhaps much, much smaller."

The naughtiness in her eyes was pretty much all Jeff needed to convince him that he could afford to take a break. Besides, he had been in the kitchen early, as was the case most days. They were as ready for dinner as they possibly could be. So with that, he bounded up the stairs after he put affairs in order with his sous chef and line cooks.

"Well hello, big man," Angela had already stripped down to the bare essentials by the time he entered their place. "Guess what I have on the menu this afternoon?"

THE PERFECT MEAL

"Popcorn and a video? I know how much you love to cuddle up with me eating popcorn and watching movies."

"And what makes you think I'd want to cuddle up with you today?"

"Possibly the fact that you have no clothes on?"

"In that case, what makes you think I'd want to watch a movie and eat popcorn?"

She was getting slinkier with ever word, but in a tasteful, sexy way. Jeff knew it was over for him so he simply grabbed a hold of her as she jumped into his arms. Wrapping athletic legs around his waist, and holding tight, they headed for the bedroom. As they embraced it was Angela's kissing that caused Jeff to misjudge passage through the bedroom door. Slightly off balance, he crashed into the jam. They both heard a cracking sound.

"Uh oh. Did I cause that, Chef Walker?"

"Bad, bad, bad girl. You've broken my meat thermometer. You will have to be punished now."

With that Jeff proceeded to punish Angela in the most severe terms possible: an hour plus of lovemaking. Not being the masochistic type, she thought that if this was punishment, she might want to break things more often.

After they had finished, Angela thought again of telling Jeff about the letters. "You probably have seen the airmail I've received from Greg since I moved in. I just wanted to share with you that he's been sending them to me."

"Should I be concerned? I don't want you running away and moving to Paris to be with him."

"Ha ha, Mr. Walker. No, he has just been a friend. I haven't actually written him back, but think I will just because it seems the right thing to do. Ever since that first encounter with him, I have to admit he's not been a terrible fellow."

"Not as terrible as me?" Jeff reached out to smack her bare ass as she leaned over for a bag she had at bedside.

"Ouch! Definitely not as terrible as you. Brat." She handed him the wooden box with the meat thermometer and the note Greg had sent with it.

"What's this?"

"Greg sent me this antique meat thermometer. Go ahead, read the note. He's just trying so hard to get me to forgive him. I think I should, but I wanted you to be aware so we had no secrets."

Taking a few moments to read the note, Jeff thought it sounded very much like Greg. "Seems harmless enough to me. I think deep down he's an okay guy. Could have been a man and told me about school. Of course, I guess it really doesn't matter that much in the long run."

"Why don't you use the thermometer until you get yourself a new one. I know a good chef should never be without his tools. You are a good chef, right?"

That comment elicited yet another loud smacking of his bare, naked lady's back side.

"Hey now! Most definitely not as terrible as you. I think your kitchen is calling you, Chef Walker. Oh, please throw me a bag of frozen peas on your way out."

If that was what they referred to as afternoon delight, he was very much in favor of it. As was usually the case after their lovemaking, he was energized and felt a deepening of the bond between himself and Angela. He liked where they were heading. As long as the talk of marriage and kids didn't pop up any time soon, he felt confident they were going to have a nice time together.

Eventually Jeff did want a deeper commitment, but he knew there was much he had to accomplish with his career. Besides, the two of them were still young and had a lot of time to make those things happen. His parents had not given birth to him until they were into their 30's. He had plenty of time to consider such things.

Just to be a smart ass, Jeff tossed Angela a bag of frozen vegetables. It was one of the few things besides beer he had in the fridge. He straightened his chef's coat, aligned his apron and made sure the antique thermometer he was borrowing from Angela was deep in the shoulder pocket holder. What he failed to notice was the little extra shimmer emanating from the gem on the gauge's dial face. Perhaps old Chef Didier's spell was finally coming to fruition.

Putting on the finishing touches to his uniform, his pager went off. The caller ID told him it was from the kitchen phone downstairs.

"Chef. You might want to get down here. Just got a call for reservations from a New York Times restaurant critic. He was using an alias but the hostess recognized the name. You better get down here, and quick."

14 PURSUIT OF THE PERFECT MEAL

Jeff punched the elevator button but simply could not wait for it to arrive. He bolted down two flights of stairs, nearly tripping at the bottom landing. Entering the kitchen through the back hall door, he looked around to get a general feel of things.

"Hey Jonny. What's the scoop? Anything more on the critic coming tonight? I've never knowingly cooked for a critic, much less one from the Times."

"Nothing more at this point, Chef. But if you're planning on offering up those specials we talked about earlier, we might want to get into gear and get them working."

"Right, right. You jump on the bisque and I'll start prepping the meat. And make sure everyone has their mis en place in place and ready. We have a booked house tonight. The last thing we need is to perform perfectly for the critic who doesn't want us to know he's here but treat everyone else like crap. No can do."

"No can do. Aye Chef!"

Off Jonny went to get the intricacies of the soon to be famous lobster bisque humming along. Focusing on the meat prep, Greg allowed his thoughts to meander from his work back a few moments to his time upstairs with Angela. He knew he was still young and rather inexperienced in both love and sex, but he was really liking his time with her. Physically, they seemed to fit together. Emotionally, he knew they had a lot of growing and maturing to do, but that was what life was all about. You just had to get from here to there, and hopefully enjoy the process along the way.

With dinner orders flowing in for nearly an hour and a half, and the kitchen well ahead of them, Jeff was finding his element as the lead chef of his kitchen. Putting out a hundred covers in an evening during the middle of the week was nothing new, and in fact he welcomed the rush to keep him from fretting about creating a great meal for the critic.

He was jarred back to the present when the expediter shouted out the next order and followed it with, "Oh, and Chef? I think this order is for that certain someone special." He winked at Jeff and went about his duties.

"All righty then. Jonny, get that bisque moving. Make sure you warm up that bowl. These guys live to rip us new ones if we blow it by not giving them hot soup in a warm bowl."

"Hot soup, warm bowl. Yes, Chef!" Jonny was as excited about this opportunity as his chef was, but he was still a professional. He had watched Jeffrey Walker grow faster than anyone he had ever worked with in a kitchen and would do everything in his power as the right hand man to make sure the review they received on tonight's dinner was top notch, first class.

Per the critics request, he took his salad after the bisque. Jeff was not one of those cooks who had to peak out the window into the dining room to watch for reactions to his food. At the same time, he definitely welcomed the updates flowing back to the kitchen from the wait staff.

"Seemed to love the soup, chef. He mentioned it was smooth as silk, rich and creamy."

"Good, good. Let's keep it going folks. This is a big fish in our little pond. Let's get him good and fat tonight."

Everything felt perfect to him as the dishes kept going out. He had pulled out the meat to let it rest and inserted the beautiful, antique thermometer to check for medium rare.

Noticing the light bouncing off the gauge dial, Jonny commented to Jeff. "New thermometer, chef? Cannot say I've seen anything quite like that before."

"Yeah, Angela and I, uhm, well, let's just say my digital one broke and she let me borrow this one till I get mine replaced. Now get back to work," he chuckled as the two cooks bent over their food in preparation of the final courses for this important meal.

When the last tickets had gone out, and the critic was no longer in the dining room, the kitchen brigade let out a few whoops and hollers. Jeff gathered the team and made a brief speech to them.

"First off, let me thank all of you for coming together so amazingly tonight. Most of you know we had a very important critic in-house and the work you all did to make that man's experience perfect was simply amazing. Not only did we serve him a nearly flawless meal, but every other patron was also provided with food and service befitting of at least a Michelin starred restaurant."

THE PERFECT MEAL

Someone in the back of the gathered crowd shouted, "Two stars, Chef!" Everyone cheered in agreement.

"I'm pretty sure he only has good things to write about us folks, but you never know. This is a crazy, crazy business. No matter what we read in tomorrow's paper, just know that if you did your very best, that's all which matters. Now, unless I'm mistaken, those tables are not going to clear themselves, the dirty dishes are not self-cleaning, and the floors will not be mopped by me tonight. Get to work, and then get out of here and enjoy your evening. Tomorrow is another day, and we'll want a repeat performance. If you have it in you!"

Jeff left the crew to finish and went upstairs. Stopping on the second floor he could hardly wait to share the news with his parents. Knocking on their door, he was called in by his mother.

"Hello, dear. How was dinner service tonight? How many covers did you all do?"

She was sitting with his father in the living room. From the looks of it, they had both been reading and listening to some soft jazz. Raymond Walker was not looking all that good. Even through several surgeries to help correct some of the burn damage, it just seemed as if his energy was low, and there was less of a spark of life in his eyes.

"Didn't anyone tell you guys? We had that critic from the Times come in under an alias. Fortunately the hostess has a friend at a place across town that had been reviewed recently. She knew a few of the names this fellow might make reservations under, so we sort of were prepared for his visit."

"And how do you think you did, son? Everything go as planned?"

"Better, Pop. Not only did we kill his meal, but everything else in the restaurant seemed to just flow perfectly all night. Nothing to distract him from the great food we put out. I'm hopeful that we're going to get an amazing review."

Apparently the smoke inhalation which had caused damage to Ray's lungs and esophagus had more permanent effects than his doctors had initially indicated. As he started to respond the coughing which ensued caused as much pain in his wife and son as it seemed to in him.

Finally, "Pardon me. I need to stop smoking. Oh, wait, I don't smoke." Still the joker, even if an old and tired one. "That's wonderful news, Jeffrey. I'm proud of you and will be regardless of what we read tomorrow. Of course, I can't speak for your mother, so for all our sakes keep your fingers crossed for a big thumbs up. Does this reviewer do that? Or is it the forks guy? 3 forks up? 2 forks down?"

"You're right Raymond. But if Jeff gets any forks down, I'm personally going to take it out of your hide. Goofball."

"But I'm your goofball, right?" He leaned over to kiss his wife, but before his lips could reach her cheek, he started in on the coughing again.

"I'd better head off to bed, son. This is great news, great news indeed. We are very proud of you, aren't we, Ruth?

"Well, I know I am. Come on honey, let me help you into the bedroom."

Not wanting to get overly emotional and sad about his father, Jeff's mood was somewhat subdued as he took the stairs up one floor to his place. Angela was there and seemed to be concealing something on their kitchen table. He had barely opened the door when she yelled out to him.

"Close your eyes Chef Walker. Close them. Keep them closed!" In a flash she was at the doorway with her hands up over his eyes. Closing the door, she guided him over to the kitchen where she told him to count to three and then open his eyes.

"One. Two. Three," looking directly ahead at the table he saw a multi-tiered cake with a great big star on the top, candles on the second level, and some words scripted on the bottom, "Congratulations Chef. Let's Eat!"

The melancholy from visiting his parents slipped away as he and Angela enjoyed the cake. There was a lot of it. The rest of the staff would have cake for lunch tomorrow.

While physically and mentally worn out, there was a definite sugar rush coming on.

"You know Ms. Harris, while the substitute thermometer you provided me was an adequate stand-in for tonight's very important service, I still believe there is a bit more punishment due for your bad, bad behavior earlier."

"Oh my, Chef Walker. More punishment? However shall I get through it all?"

He wasn't sure exactly how much he had doled out to her before they had drifted off to sleep. While he was completely enraptured after the two had simultaneously climaxed in an emotional and physical culmination, the only thing he could focus on while watching her sleep was what the critic would say about his food.

How long had he been waiting for this moment to arrive? It was just a few hours away now, but seemed like an eternity. It could only be good news, right? As his mind fought to continue worrying about the review, his tired body gave in, forcing all of him to drift off to a deep, relaxed sleep.

Being on the third floor, and in the back of the building, Jeff would never have heard the newspaper being delivered just a few hours later. But his parents, now early bird risers were waiting in the dining room with a pot of coffee. They saw their paper boy ride by with his bike, tossing today's news casually up to the restaurant. Ruth unlocked the front door and reached for the papers outside. It was time for the parents to learn just how good their son was.

15 REVIEW IS IN

Not wanting to wake her son, Ruth slipped the Times food section under Jeff's door after she had read the critic's review out loud to Raymond. She had wanted to wait for the young adults to come down for breakfast, but Ray was far too impatient for that to happen.

Angela retrieved the newspaper and after making coffee, put it and some mugs on a tray and proceeded to provide in bed delivery.

"Wakey, wakey, eggs and bakey."

Jeff stirred a bit and finally rolled over as Angela poured coffee about twelve inches from his face. "You made eggs, bacon and coffee for breakfast? Wowser. Maybe this living together thing really is a good idea."

"Don't get used to it mister. No eggs. No bacon. Just coffee. When was the last time we had any real food in the fridge up here? Silly. Your mother delivered the newspaper under our front door. I thought that was wonderful of her."

Jeff popped up in the bed and scootched himself up against the headboard. Angela snuggled up under the covers next to him and waited patiently for him to have his first sip of coffee.

"Oh, come on already, Chef Walker. Get to the review section, will you?"

Just for that, Jeff slowed down, took a long draw on his mug of Java and casually glanced over the front page of the food section. Angela balled up her fist in front of his stomach.

"I will gut punch you buddy. Come on!"

"Okay, okay. Boy talk about having no patience whatsoever."

Turning pages until he found the new reviews, Jeff saw where his restaurant had been critiqued and folded the paper back on itself, then down in half, and finally over to one quarter of its original size. He had performed this in a slow and deliberate fashion to take even more time for the dramatic effect of making Angela wait. Finally, he started reading. Silently, to himself.

"Out loud, you bum." She gave him a medium strength socking to the midsection.

He could not help but laugh out loud, "Stop it, you. Okay, here we go." He went on to read the review to her. Hardly a word had been written which could be interpreted as anything other than positive. The reviewer commented on how professional and courteous the front of house staff had been, not only to him but the other patrons observed during his visit.

"I knew our wait staff would do an excellent job. Right on."

The reviewer proceed to recount each course all with high praise. Finally, to summarize his meal and the culinary mind behind it, he spoke directly about Chef Walker.

Jeff read this verbatim to Angela. "One would be hard pressed to find a more talented and passionate young cook in the area. Chef Walker's attention to detail is superb. His ability to blend the flavors of just a few ingredients to produce such complexity in the finished dish seems advanced for his age. All in all, the food was quite good, and one should certainly consider visiting this up and coming new chef. Be aware however that it is still very early on in his career and I do feel there is some room for improvement. While wonderful, it could not be called the perfect meal. There is however, in Chef Walker's case, plenty of time for that to happen should he stay on his current course."

Angela was ecstatic. She wrapped both arms around his waist, her head buried in his chest and squeezed him with all she had.

Overall, Jeff was basically satisfied with what had been written of the meal, but that last little bit of "advice" struck him as odd.

"Why do you think he said that about my food not being the perfect meal?"

"I don't know sweetheart. But don't focus on that. Look at everything else he mentioned and how good he felt it all was. Can you imagine the affect this is going to have on business? I'll never see you once the foodies get a hold of this."

"Maybe, but still. I don't get it. Why even mention that it wasn't a perfect meal if you liked so much about it? What the hell is the perfect meal anyway?"

Angela was concerned about where Jeff was placing his focus. Clearly this reviewer had enjoyed the food, and the ambiance. Why focus on the single comment in the whole article that might be interpreted as less than positive?

"I think you're wonderful, and so will every person on the planet who reads that review. You'll see, Chef Walker, you'll see. I have to get up and get ready. I'd like to get a run in before work. Don't let yourself be consumed, honey. Okay?"

"No, you're right Angela. It was mostly good news. I'm alright." The truth was, he was not happy with being told his food was good but not perfect. As he watched his girlfriend leave his bed and head for the bathroom, he failed to see the beautiful young woman before him. He could only see his next culinary goal in life. Producing the perfect meal.

THE PERFECT MEAL

.

16 WORK, WORK, WORK

For the ensuing few months both Jeff and Angela could do nothing but focus on their respective careers and businesses. The Times review had indeed struck a chord with the ever curious foodies in the City. The restaurant had even started getting an increased number of visitors from much further away than just the 5 boroughs. The extra reservations forced Jeff to extend both the lunch and dinner services. It was now routine for them to take orders until midnight. Raymond always told Jeff that when the picking is good, you have to get to work harvesting the bounty.

Harris Supplies had also been doing quite well. In less than a year Angela had increased business by nearly 50% which required much more time and energy. She had needed to replace one of the older delivery vehicles and decided that was a good time to expand the delivery areas, which required a new truck.

Plus there was the new staff she would have to hire and train. All this sapped her but she was grateful for the opportunity to be doing so well. The very last thing she would do is let down her uncle, or her father. So, she tended to stay in the office after regular business hours with paperwork, preparing the next days deliveries, and generally doing all the stuff that she would have to pay someone else overtime to complete.

Angela would get home between 9 and 11 pm most work days. She was thankful that being a house maiden was not part of the relationship she had with Jeff. The years of taking care of her ailing father had pretty much cured her of wanting to do that again anytime soon.

Prior to her father getting ill and becoming bed bound, Angela had provided care for her mother. A lovely woman struck with terminal breast cancer when Angela was just thirteen. She wasted away for five years before passing on. Essentially all of Angela's teen years had been devoted to providing for the dying woman, feeding her father and keeping the household tidy.

Her high school graduation held only the promise of more of the same. When Mrs. Harris passed relatively suddenly, Angela realized she was free. Maybe she could even consider going to college. There had been a few small schools interested in her joining their long distance running team, and her grades were superb as well.

Some days guilt would take over. The relief Angela had felt once her mother died would get pounded into the pavement on daily runs. This usually measured itself in the form of several extra miles. After almost three months the guilt began to subside. Missing her mother set in. She was perfectly fine with that feeling.

It was mid-summer when the unimaginable happened. A college had been selected. Paperwork submitted. The only thing left was to spend a final few months at home with her father.

Her departing project was to ensure nothing would keep him from being able to sustain himself. Laundry and simple cooking lessons ensued. It was some of the closest time she had ever spent with her father.

His diagnosis of lung cancer, well into stage three floored them both. The guilt she felt at her mother's passing immediately told her there would be no college. Not that year. Not for several years, in fact.

Angela deeply loved her father and provided him the best care she could. But she hated every second of every day until he too, passed away.

Of course, she cared about Jeff and wanted to be there for him emotionally. Since he ate most of his meals in his own restaurant's kitchen he did not rely on her to cook. She would do a good amount of cleaning their apartment, but he pitched in after he woke up in the late mornings before heading to work.

As obsessed as ever with garnering that perfect meal moniker, Jeff was slowly, almost imperceptibly zoning everything and most everyone out of his tunneled vision. Since Angela had been spending a lot of time with her business he felt little obligation to work much on the continuing development of their relationship. There was one person who paid attention to all of this. Ruth decided she needed to say something to someone, and since most of her time was spent caring for her husband, Ray was chosen. She just needed to get his his focus off the television.

"Raymond Walker. Honey. Do you think you might be able to live without one hour of following the exploits of that Captain James Kirk and talk with me? I know you've not been able to get out much lately dear, but have you noticed how single minded Jeffrey has become? He's spending a lot of time working in those kitchens or preparing to work in them. I don't know when the last time he and Angela simply took some time off and got away from things around here."

Raymond's health was in steady decline. He still had a bit of wry humor about him, but Ruth could tell he was never going to be his energetic, jovial self again. She just continued to love him and provide the best care and companionship a wife could and should for her soul mate.

"They're young and filled with ambitions, Ruthie. I seem to recall being a bit focused when we opened up this joint as well. I will admit that having you here working with me probably helped solidify the relationship we had then."

"And what about the relationship we have now, Mr. Walker?"

"Oh, yeah, that one too," he winked at her as she feigned being upset. "We are very lucky, Mrs. Walker, to have lived together for so long, and loved each other so deeply. Well, I can only speak for myself. I cannot imagine a man having a more perfect life than the one I've enjoyed. Even with the accident and my spiraling health, I feel showered with your love and affection every moment of every day. If things are right for those crazy kids, they'll get to that point as well."

"Perhaps you're right. I just get worried seeing Jeffrey work so hard, so late every night. I've also noticed the past few months that Angela seems to come home from her office quite late as well. I just wonder when they are ever finding time to do anything other than fall asleep together and wake up to part from each other every day. Seems tragic if you ask me."

"Come now Ruth, let them live their own lives. Just love them like you do, and leave them be."

------ oOo ------

It was the very rare occasion that both Jeff and Angela found themselves alone in their apartment before midnight. As usual Jeff had been reflecting on the day's services and was finding every little detail he could nit pick about why the food might not be considered perfect. Not wanting to be sucked into yet another of his self-analysis, Angela hoped they might talk about anything other than work.

"I'm sure you're being overly critical Jeff. Look at all the great reviews you have gotten these past months since that first one. The foodies love you, the professionals love you, and I can't even count how many reviewers have had nothing but amazing things to say about your food."

"Angela, you just don't understand how tough it is. I cannot let up, not even for a moment. I know, deep in my gut, that when I allow something less than perfect to go out, it's going to be to the wrong customer, and I'll be sunk. Don't you get that? I've worked too hard to let that happen."

She felt his passions but was concerned about the fact he was increasing his obsession over that comment.

"So what is the current status with the Food Network folks? You mentioned a couple of weeks ago some of their producers had come by to chat with you at lunch. Have you heard anything more from them?"

"No, nothing. I'm sure they are simply waiting to see if I flub things up and start letting garbage go out on my plates."

Biting her tongue, deciding it better not to pursue the hope of peaceful conversation that evening, Angela simply got up from the couch and kissed him on the cheek.

"I'm heading to bed. There's some extra deliveries coming for the new area in the morning and I'll need to be there early to help coordinate. Don't sit here all night lamenting about things. Okay?"

He muttered a reply, "Okay, okay." Of course, he proceeded to sit there drinking beers until he fell asleep on the couch.

Angela left the apartment quietly the next morning. She had not particularly cared for his mood the night before, and was even less satisfied with the patterns they had fallen into of late. His passion and directed focus were great, however there was something off with his attitude. All this perfect meal stuff was getting to her.

As Angela passed through the dining room, Ruth called out, "Come have some coffee with me Angela. I've not spent any time with you in forever. How are you dear?"

The early part of the day was Ruth's sole domain as her husband usually slept in most mornings. His sleeping patterns were severely affecting any real rest either of them were able to attain. She had even moved to another bedroom so as not to be a source of agitation for him. As a result, she enjoyed the quiet restaurant until deliveries and lunch preparations kicked off.

"Oh, Mrs. Walker. I would love some coffee. Yes, please. I'm doing fine. Busy with the delivery business, but I won't complain about being successful on that front. I just hope I'm doing father and my uncle proud."

"I'm certain you are, dear. Staying busy and focused can be a good thing. Speaking of being focused, how is that son of mine? I think I see him even less than I see you."

"Well, Ruth, you speak of focus, and that barely begins to describe where Jeff's head and heart have been. Do you remember when he got that first critic's review? How great it all was, but for that one comment about his dinner not being the perfect meal?"

"Of course I do. How has Jeff been dealing with that?"

"I think it's safe to say he has become obsessed. Don't get me wrong, I love him for his dedication and passion. Clearly with all the great reviews and press he's been receiving, he's doing amazing things in his kitchen. But...," her voice trails off as she searched for a way to share more with Ruth.

THE PERFECT MEAL

"But what, Angela? What more is there, honey?" Ruth holds her hands waiting for the rest.

"I, I don't know Ruth. Something seems to be missing now. In fact, it feels as if we have less every day. Maybe I'm just imagining things. I truly hope I am, but I fear the worst. My biggest concerns is that I'm not seeing things as they truly are between us. Please don't say anything to Jeff about this. I'm sure we'll work it through. You and Mr. Walker had tough patches, didn't you?"

"No, dear. We never had a challenge. Never raised our voices. We always lived in perfect harmony together." She could only smile after that performance.

"Are you making fun, Mrs. Walker?"

"Of course I am, dear. Yes, we had our spells. But we made it through. All I can say in terms of support and advice is to just continue to love each other, best you can. Both Ray and I are firm believers that if things are meant to be, they'll work out. You'll find a way through these challenges. And if you don't, always try to remain on friendly terms. You are both beautiful young people with your entire lives ahead of you. The very last thing you need is to have large blocks of negative emotions clogging up that future."

On the verge of tears, Angela managed a smile. "Thank you Ruth. You are like a mother to me. Thank you so much." She leaned over the table, kissing the woman on the cheek. "Oh, how is Mr. Walker doing these days?"

Ruth paused, sighing, "Not well, dear. I fear the downhill slope is becoming more slippery each day."

Still holding Ruth's hands, Angela felt impelled to offer her help and support. "That's terrible. I am so sorry for you both. Is there anything I can do?"

"That is so sweet of you. You know, it would be a true blessing to get a few hours alone in the afternoon now and then. I hate to ask you for your free time when you're not working. But it would mean the world to me. Maybe on the weekends? You wouldn't have to do much other than just being there with him."

Before Ruth finished making the request years of memories came to the forefront of Angela's consciousness. What seemed like wasted years providing home health care for two dying parents streamed before her. And then the years of guilt and regret for the way she felt after their passing.

Her running, healthy eating and focus on taking care of herself was the only way she could battle the haunting emotions. No one would ever have to provide her with care at any point of her life.

"Oh, Angela, honey. I am sorry for asking. The look on your face tells me all I need to know. It was careless of me to think you might want to spend time with Jeff's father. Please, please forgive me."

"No, Ruth, you must forgive me. I was just remembering my mother and father. Towards the end of both their lives I would have given my soul to find a few hours of solace and solitude. Of course I will be able to give you a break on the weekends. It would be an honor and my complete pleasure. Besides, Mr. Walker is a riot!"

"Oh you are an angel aren't you? Just don't let him suck you into watching too much of that Star Trek."

------ oOo ------

Sipping her coffee while she walked briskly down the block towards the subway, Angela turned to look back over her left shoulder and across the street. For some reason, she had the feeling of being watched. When she looked over towards the front of the Anderson's restaurant, she saw nothing. No one was there.

It was not until the light changed and she was crossing the street and turning the corner she noticed him. Now gazing over her right shoulder as she turned to head down the stairwell, she felt the urge to look up at the windows above Anderson's. There, following her every move from one of the third floor windows, he had been watching as she left Walker's and made her way down the street.

Somewhat caught off guard, Angela could only wave briefly as she descended into the subway station. Greg Anderson was unsure if she had seen him wave back.

------ oOo ------

Greg's flight from Paris had gotten in late the night before. He was so glad to be home, back in New York. His good fortune in catching a brief glimpse of Angela let him know that life was good. Ever since she started writing to him, they had developed a friendship and he looked forward to spending time with her in person, not just through the written words on thin, translucent, airmail paper.

Before any of that was going to happen, however, he needed to touch bases with his father and see where he was going to fit into the scheme of things around the kitchen. Downstairs Greg found Gerald having coffee, reading the morning paper in the lounge.

"Hello Father. Surprised to see me?"

"Why son, good morning to you. My you look fit and ready to go. Seems your time in France might have done you some good after all. Also seems you've been neglecting to support a Parisian barber! How are you feeling today?"

"Great, dad, just great. School was amazing. I learned so much about food and cooking there I just hope I'm able to put it all to good use back here in our kitchens. How's Mother? I didn't want to wake her if she wasn't already up."

THE PERFECT MEAL

"Your mother is wonderful, as always. We just got back from a little mini-vacation and are both recharged and ready to go. While we were away we decided that you should immediately become our new sous chef and start preparing to take over the Executive position. My understanding is that whenever we all feel you're ready to go, our current exec will happily leave."

"Why would he do that, Dad? I don't wish to push anyone out of their job."

"You won't be son. Trust me. He's been threatening to quit the line and write that cook book he's always dreamed of. The way I see, the faster you pick it all up and take over the reigns, the better he'll feel about getting on and pursuing his own dreams and aspirations."

"Well, in that case, you can count on me to put in 110%. I know there's a lot I have to learn, but I really feel this is what I'm supposed to be doing with my life. The people I met at school and while in Paris really opened up my heart and soul to food and cooking. I might have seemed somewhat indifferent when I left here, and if so, I trust you and Mother will accept my apologies. I also don't think I'll ever be able to thank you enough for pushing me in the right direction. I guess you knew what you were doing to me."

Gerald had been waiting for the moment when he would find connection, respect and appreciation from his son. Seems as if it had descended upon him this morning when he had least expected it. Since his time spent with Ray Walker, and the one on one time with Betty, Gerald's attitude had softened immensely. Upon hearing these words from Greg, he could only stand up, reach out to his son, and give him the hug which he'd been holding onto for years.

"Thank you, Gregory. Today you have made me a very happy, proud father. And I like your hair, don't worry." Several tears trickled down his face as he held onto his son's embrace for just a few moments longer.

17 FRIENDS AGAIN FOR THE FIRST TIME

Steadily focusing on improving his craft, Jeff tended to skip opportunities to spend time with his girlfriend and others who once had been important parts of his life. Angela had been working extremely hard with her business but was still coming home as early as she could, trying also to set up her days so that she need not be at the office before the sun came up. Unfortunately, the nature of the food industry simply would not allow complete control of ones schedule.

Even so, the more she attempted to make time for him, the more Jeff seemed unable to share that time. As a result, Angela had the opportunity to go out with her girlfriends and even had the occasional instance to be in Greg Anderson's company. Apparently he valued taking regular time off from his restaurant duties and would always call Angela to try and fit himself into her schedule.

As these friendly interactions increased, Angela had begun to open up more to Greg, sharing the current state of affairs in her relations with Jeff.

"I am beginning to get really bummed out by how little he seems to want spend time with me, Greg. Just don't understand how we went from sneaking afternoons in bed together to quite honestly, and I'm sorry to be blunt, having no sex at all."

Greg knew much of what was motivating Jeff now that the role in his own restaurant was growing. "Working in this life is intoxicating, alluring, and addictive. When you are as good as he is, you're constantly under pressure. A lot of pressure, Angela. I know you understand, right? At least intellectually?"

Of course Greg would know the perfectly right thing to say.

"Yes, I intellectually understand where Jeff's head and heart is." She used finger quotes when she spoke of intellectual understanding. "But damn it, I don't get it emotionally. Why do you choose to spend time with me when you could be working away in your kitchen?"

"Because you're my friend? And that's what friends do for each other. They make time to just be there. How was that answer? Win me any brownie points?" he smiled while giving her a little pinch on her bicep.

"Ouch," she slugged him back in the arm. "It did, but you lost them for such a wimpy pinch. But yeah, I hear you, I really do. Almost every part of my body screams for me to slap myself for being such a selfish bitch and not respecting Jeff for the dedication to his career. The only part that fights against all that rage is my heart. It stands up for me saying things like I should desire someone who will make at least as much time for me as I do for him. It also says silly stuff like I can respect his career and still expect to be treated like I'm in a loving relationship. Constant internal battle Gregory. Constant, I tell you."

It would be so very easy for Greg to jump in between his friend and his ex-best friend. Nothing would make him happier than having her recognize how much he cares for her, not only as a friend, but deeper down, as much more. But he just could not sink to that level of manipulation. Much as he wanted the brass ring, he had changed the way he dealt with others during his time in France. He could only sit by holding vigil with his friend as she processed life and her love for one, Jeffrey Walker.

"You can always hang out here with all your other friends. We have most of Walker's employees hang out here after dinner. In fact, our little bar is becoming quite the local after hours, industry hot spot. You, my dear friend, are welcome to drink away your troubles any night of the week. Except Wednesday nights."

"And what happens on Wednesday nights?"

"We're experimenting with poetry readings. Seems there are still a lot of folks that like to listen to hippy types reading strange, whacked out words they call poetry. Cool thing for us, those same folks tend to spend money on booze, coffee, appetizers and various other snacks. Ends up being quite profitable, even if the poetry is far out there."

"Well, that sounds delightful. I may have to pull up a stool and start snapping my fingers one Wednesday night just to check it out."

"You are more than welcome any time, day or night. Why don't you try and snag that boyfriend of yours for next week? I have a bit of pull around here, so I might be able to reserve you a good table."

"I should hope so. It's the least you could do for a friend as good as me." She smiled and reached out to squeeze his hand for a brief moment.

It was these innocent interactions which cranked amperage through Greg's heart and soul. Of course, he could only react as a male friend was expected. He smiled back as he replied, "Great friend. As great a friend like you."

He continued to smile just the right way.

------ oOo ------

Seeing the sliver of light from the living room grow as Jeff opened their bedroom door, Angela made the effort to focus on the bedside clock. Nearly 1:30 a.m. She was groggy, but really wanted to give Jeff enough notice to make sure he would clear his calendar for next week.

"Did you know that the Anderson's have an open mic poetry night on Wednesdays? Greg was telling me about it tonight."

"Must be nice to have all that extra space to be able to do interesting things other than cook great food," Jeff responded to her, irritated at the mention of Greg.

"Don't you think he is a good cook? I've eaten his food several times since he's come back from school and I think there is a lot of talent in that boy."

Tired, Jeff becomes somewhat dismissive of her, "I'm sure you're right. He is a culinary school graduate so I'm sure his skills are far superior to anyone else in the near vicinity."

"That's not what I meant, Jeff. What's the matter with you? I just thought it might be nice for us to take some time off and spend a lovely evening doing something interesting and different. Greg told me that a lot of food service folks hang out in their bar after hours, but not on Wednesday when they do the poetry stuff."

"Uh, huh." His complete lack of desire to engage frustrated her.

Reaching out to turn on the bed side lamp she confronted him. "Why won't you make time for me any more, Jeff? Don't you consider us important? Are you that narrow minded that continuing to have a loving relationship with me is no longer of interest to you? What the hell is going on Jeff Walker?" The steady rise in her volume irritated him even more.

He felt certain that if he did not make some sort of concession to her right now, this tirade was not going to end any time in the near future. After a heavy, slow sigh, "I'll do what I can to make sure that I'm able to get off next Wednesday evening. It'll have to be after 9 p.m., though. I trust that will meet with your satisfaction?"

"Fine," she blurted out while reaching to turn off the lamp. She turned her back to him as he was getting into bed and pulling up the sheet and covers. "Fine," she said again with almost as much emphasis. It only took those few seconds for exhaustion to pull Jeff into immediate sleep. He missed the frustration in her voice.

------ oOo ------

THE PERFECT MEAL

When the first intermission occurred during the poetry reading, Greg left the kitchen to see if his friends had made it to their reserved table. There was only one chair occupied, and he knew immediately, even from behind that only Angela had shown up for the show. Curious, he made his way over.

"This was supposed to be a table for two, madam. Since we have a 2 drink minimum, you are now on the hook to buy at least 4 espressos."

The look on his face told Angela that she did not have to have that much caffeine. "You're a big brat Greg Anderson. I should buy them and force you to drink all that coffee. I may, however, have them set me up with 4 shots of tequila. Or is that frowned upon during these type of events?"

"Definitely frowned upon. Unless you have double that amount. And if you do that, chances are you become the event. That is very acceptable, and with very few frowns."

"Good to know what my options are. You've noticed, right?"

He had observed it immediately upon finding her sitting alone at the table.

"Uhm, your boyfriend spends a lot of time in the bathroom?"

"I wish. Try another room in the restaurant. But not your restaurant. His. Across the street where right this very moment he's the big man who absolutely cannot miss making the meal for whichever critic or foodie or wannabe writer is dangling the promise of yet more good press in front of his damned nose."

The lights dimmed before Greg had a chance to comment. Instead he simply patted her hand which had been resting on the table and gave her that friendly, understanding, and infinitely patient smile of his.

She was realizing that having Greg as a friend had turned out to be a great thing after all. As the emcee introduced the next poet, she leaned into Greg, whispering, "You just don't realize how lucky you are to be sitting here with me and not my office receptionist, Shelly."

He had no clue what that meant, but knew he would rather be sitting there with her than anyone else. It was unfortunate she and Jeff had been experiencing such turmoil. Everything else in Chef Walker's life appeared to be going so well. As is the case with much in life, Greg knew the book's cover told a far different story than the words printed on its pages.

18 THE DAYS BEFORE THE LAST SUPPER

Anderson's now former head chef removed his toque, bowed with sincerity towards Gerald and turned to depart the back of the kitchen for the last time. Watching him leave, Gerald now had the most pleasant task of informing his son the kitchen was solely his. Bypassing the cooking area, Gerald entered the dining room to see a very light crowd, and knew they would not be tearing through orders in the back. Deciding to take advantage of the lull, he located his wife and made their way to the kitchen.

"Very briefly, everyone. Everyone, gather around for just a moment. We have a quick announcement to make." Gerald waits a few moments as the kitchen brigade pull pots and pans aside, or at least reposition themselves in order to keep one eye on their food, and the other on their boss.

"Some of you may know that our head chef has been itching for some time to finish writing his cookbook. I've just been informed that he's decided that time has come and he's off to pursue his dreams of becoming an author of culinary secrets. As a result, we have a position to fill here at Anderson's."

Gerald speaks and most of the employees begin looking in Greg's general direction.

"Mrs. Anderson and I are extremely proud to announce to you our choice for executive chef is none other than our son, Gregory Anderson."

As the gathering of employees applaud, the casual observer might think Gerald had just given birth to his first born male child. Chef Greg steps up on the lower shelves of nearby food prep tables, outstretches his arms in order to gain the floor, and speaks to everyone.

"Mother, Father, thank you so very much for this opportunity. I'm pretty sure neither of you ever thought I would make it to this point, did you? Hell, I'm not sure I ever thought this day would come for me, or that I really wanted it to happen. But it is here now, and no one is happier for me than, well, me!"

Laughter and more applause. "Seriously, though. We have a great team in all of you, and my intentions are to continue the great work my folks have done to make this one of the nicest dining establishments in the City. I plan to have an open grill policy, so anything you need to talk to me about, please, don't be shy."

Greg makes his way though people towards his parents. Amidst the back slaps, and high fives, he finally reaches his mother and gets a big hug from her. Being unable to resist, Gerald hugs them both at the same time.

"I love you, Mom and Dad. I will make you proud. You have my solemn word on that."

------ oOo ------

At Gerald's suggestion, Greg starts planning a menu for his private, coming out dinner. In addition to showcasing his cooking skills, both Andersons realize this is an excellent way to get the word out about the great new chef cooking at their place. Greg will invite family, key employees, close friends and some business associates whose positive recommendations would create a nice flow of interested new customers.

In his desire to showcase all he learned while at school in France as well as his time studying locally with their previous head chef, Greg decides there are a number of ingredients he will have delivered the morning of his special meal.

"You'll have them fresh?" he asks the person on the other end of the phone for the third time. "You must get them to me, extremely fresh, that morning. If you can't it's perfectly okay, just tell me now so I can find someone else who can."

For the third time, his specialty food supplier insists there will be no problem getting his unique ingredients nor having them in his kitchen bright and early the day they will be needed.

Since this is such a momentous occasion, Gerald has decided they will close the restaurant to the regular public and only feed the special guests. He will also have plenty of staff so no diners will wait on their courses to be served. This is like a dream opportunity to Greg, and he spends every free moment developing his dishes and working on a delicious dessert to culminate his meal.

Early Saturday afternoon, between the lunch and dinner services, Greg was having a coffee in his bar area. Hunched over a yellow legal pad writing, scratching through words, and generally working out the meal plan for the party a week and a day away, he failed to hear the front doors open. Just as blind to what was going on around him, he was startled when someone suddenly placed their hands over his eyes shutting down his menu planning.

"Ah, you're very clever aren't you? Speaking no words so I cannot tell right away if you're man, woman or child." He reaches for the hands and discovers they are gloved. "Even more clever. Wearing gloves so I have trouble determining if you are a man or a woman. Or a woman with man hands."

No longer able to keep up the charade for fear her laughter will give her away, Angela removed her gloved hands from his face, and laughed heartily out loud.

"Man hands? That's hilarious. Hey, I don't have man hands do I?" she asked feigning concern while dramatically pulling off her gloves and extending her arms to inspect her hands. "Decidedly NOT!"

They both laughed now, and Greg wonders what she is up to. "How may I be of service, Manhandy?"

That elicited a mock slap across his face with her gloves. Now it is Greg's turn to fake a pained response. "You kill me. You just kill me. If we weren't friends, I can tell you this, we would definitely not be friends."

"Humbug. You would most certainly fall under my friendship spell, Chef Anderson. CHEF ANDERSON. Look at you, all grown up and cheffy now. I'm very happy for you and quite impressed."

"Well, you might want to wait and taste the food I'm going to serve next Sunday. I've been working diligently on my menu. Have all my special ingredients on order, some of which are so fresh they are going to harvest them at first light next Sunday and have them in my kitchen before they know they're no longer alive. You can't beat that, right?"

Angela pondered before replying, "Will you be cooking these unsuspecting ingredients? Or will the lucky diners get to see the expression of surprise when your ingredients realize they are no longer among the living?"

"Ah, well you'll just have to show up to find out, now won't you? Oh, bring that guy you see who has something to do with cooking or food or whatever it is he does."

Trying to get Jeff to make plans in advance is worse than pulling teeth, but she assured Greg, "I know how important this dinner is for you Greg, both personally and professionally. We don't want to fill his head any fuller, but Jeff putting in good words for you with his friends and associates would certainly do wonders as you launch your career."

"So, you are actually a good friend after all. Wow. Who would have thought it? But you are right. If I pull off an amazing meal, the best reward will be that my guests love the food and are not afraid of telling others so."

"I'm sure you'll be amazing. Don't you worry. Just remember though, when you become a powerful and famous chef, you better not forget who your friends are." She finished that statement by clenching her fists with thumbs extended and making the motion of pointing both thumbs back towards herself.

"Never, ever, ever, Ms. Harris. On that you have my word. Now get out of here so I can finish up my plans."

"You cannot kick me out. I'm leaving. I'm going home right now and start working on Chef Walker so he doesn't try and weasel out of your big party. Later gator."

Greg really did feel as if he had a great friend in Angela. Of course, he would still love to have more, but with his new position and the fact that she seemed unwilling to walk away from a relatively unhappy relationship, he could only focus on things within his control.

Watching as she walked out the door he softly called after he, "Goodbye my friend. See you soon. But never soon enough."

------ oOo ------

Nearly a year had passed since Jeff had been reviewed by the Times. It was very early Saturday morning, his mother and he were enjoying coffee while waiting for the paper to be delivered. So much had transpired over the course of those four seasons it almost seemed surreal.

For Ruth, she had to face the inevitable fact that she was about to lose the love of her life. Ray had to be readmitted to the hospital because his breathing had just become more than he could manage on his own. Now the only thing keeping him alive were machines filling his lungs with air.

"I don't want to rain on the parade, Jeffrey, but after we read your new review, I'm going to head over to spend the day with your father. His doctors don't feel he has much time left. I need to be with him for any and all of that time. I hope you'll be able to stop by today or tomorrow and check in with him. In fact, bring the review and read that to him. You know how much he loves to hear about his super star son."

"Not sure about super star, Mother, but yes, I'll get by there. Maybe not today, but I'll make time to see him tomorrow before going to Greg's dinner party."

"Oh, that's right. Dear me. Not sure if I'll talk to Betty today. Will you be so sweet as to let she and Gerald, and Greg of course, know that I would love to be there, with Raymond, but for obvious reasons that won't be happening?"

"I have no choice mother. You bore an amazingly sweet child when you and Pop had me. I'll be sure to send your regrets."

A thud at the restaurant door, and Jeff jumped up to get the paper.

------ oOo ------

The rest of Saturday came and went. Most of Greg's day was spent working on any aspect of his menu that might allow for advanced preparation. Additionally, since they would not be taking reservations the next day, many of the regular Sunday diners had decided to eat out that Saturday. Knowing they were completely booked, he had a lot of mis en place to get through for their regular business in addition to his party meal.

Angela only planned to be in her offices for half the day. Not only did she want to buy herself a new dress for Greg's dinner, but she had hoped Jeff might be able to join her in a visit to his ailing father. True to her word, she was home and ready to go to the hospital just after 1:30 p.m. Just as true to his tendencies of late, Jeff absolutely could not possibly take the time away from getting ready for the dinner rush. Something about some very important customer bringing in several out of town friends. All apparently equally as important.

Jeff had wanted to go and see his father, but early in the lunch service the manager delivered the news about the special party wanting to dine with them that evening. There was just no way he was going to be able to spend several hours away from the kitchens and get everything ready for dinner.

"Look Angela, I'm really sorry. But there's nothing I can do about it. Pop will understand. He would want me to put out perfect food for these folks. Besides, I'll make sure and go by tomorrow to see him."

The specter of perfect food there haunting their relationship yet again. She had seriously considered poisoning that food critic, but knew it would have to be somewhere else. She would not even dare imagine how that act might impact Jeff's outlook if it happened during his pursuit of the holy grail of dinner dishes.

She could only shake her head at Jeff, "Whatever Jeffrey. He's only your father. But I'm sure you know best. Speaking of," she double gulped, "perfect food, you never mentioned what the reviewer had to say in the write up today." She wasn't sure that bringing this up was good or not, but at this point her ability to really care was diminishing drastically.

"Same thing mostly. Great this. Wonderful that. Blah, blah, blah. At least this time he had the decency to leave out mention of my food not standing up to his perfect meal stature."

"But you're still obsessed with making that perfect meal, aren't you?"

Jeff knew this conversation would lead to the usual ending. They fight, he leaves, she gets sad. He figured it might be best just to leave and forgo the waste of energy on the fight and dealing with her sadness later.

"I've got to get back down to the kitchen. Please tell my father I'll stop by tomorrow to see him. What time do we need to head across the street for dinner?"

"5:30 should be fine. I'll be sure to tell your father."

For the first time since things really had begun souring between the young couple, Angela didn't feel much like fighting or getting sad about the state of affairs. She watched somewhat dispassionately as Jeff left the apartment. She started considering what might be next. With these thoughts on her mind she left to visit Raymond.

Ruth was making her way down the hall as Angela approached Ray's room. Sensing that the young woman was somewhat out of her normal sorts, she inquired.

"Nothing Mrs. Walker, just more of the same thing with Jeff. He won't come today to see his father because of work. He won't really talk with me anymore about anything. It's all very frustrating, and I fear things are no longer working out between us."

Contemplating the situation Ruth replied, "Maybe you two can have some real conversation tomorrow at Gregory's dinner party. That should be a nice chance for him to let his own pressures go."

"Would you tell him to leave the Walker restaurant thoughts at Walker's restaurant when we leave tomorrow?"

"I can certainly mention it to him dear, if you think it will help."

"Honestly? I hope it's like pointing to the other end of the hallway, down there, and asking you not to think about the herd of pink elephants charging in our direction."

------ oOo ------

Sleeping in was not a luxury Jeff enjoyed very often. He had actually arranged to have the entire day off because of Greg's dinner. Being unconscious he failed to recognize the irony of not having his girlfriend around in order to take advantage of some free, alone time together. Being asleep, he also failed to hear his phone ring or his pager go off. Of course, the pager was on vibrate and still in last night's dirty chef's jacket.

The voice mail was brief. "Jeffrey, it's you mother. I'm rushing to the hospital. They just called saying you father has had a sudden, extreme change in his condition. I'm really scared for him, dear. I'm going over right now in the company mini-van. I didn't want you to think anything had happened to it should you not see it later. Call me soon as you get this and I'll fill you in with whatever I know."

Having been in such a panic, Ruth only picked up the keys to the van and left immediately after calling Jeff. She failed to pick up her purse, or even take a wallet with money and ID. She had one single focus. She needed to get to Raymond's side and hold his hand. Immediately.

With a bit of tunnel vision and tears in her eyes the speed Ruth Walker drove at was probably not advisable. She knew the inevitable was fast approaching and if she could get that van to move quick enough, she might be able to win the race to be with Ray first. She was mostly fortunate that it was early Sunday morning with traffic lighter than normal. She was mostly fortunate, but not completely.

19 LAST SUPPER

Though trying to fight back his anger, Greg is pissed off that his specially ordered ingredients never arrived. He called the delivery company's offices, however being Sunday, there was no answer. He could only leave a message.

"I thought your company was going to deliver fresh ingredients to my restaurant first thing this morning. Damn it! The only thing worse than you delivering stale, old food to me is NOT DELIVERING MY DAMNED FOOD AT ALL!"

He really wanted to say more, but his senses came back around. He really hoped they heard how hard he slammed the phone down.

"Nothing to be done about that now," he was muttering to himself. "I'll just have to take that dish off the menu. Maybe I can find a suitable replacement with stock I have on hand. Hmmm…"

He could not dwell on that which he had no control any longer, so he went about reworking things and moving his masterpiece meal forward. Passing by the chef's offices, Gerald caught the phone message his son had left the supplier as well as his self-talk afterward. He wanted to go in and discuss the matter, but felt his son had been dealt a blow and had reacted accordingly. His boy was going to do just fine taking over the business.

Having visited Ray for longer than she expected on Saturday, Angela decided to grab Greg's little sister to find a dress first thing Sunday morning. She and Lizbeth's shopping adventure had been quite fruitful. Angela had no idea what a lovely and competent young woman Greg's little sister had become. As a reward, she left Angela with not one but two pairs of shoes. Having a keen eye for fashion and being articulate enough to tell Angela when something didn't fit or look good was a true inspiration in the selection of a great dress for the evening's festivities.

THE PERFECT MEAL

Being late in the afternoon as she made her way back into the apartment, she was struck by the fact Jeff was still asleep in their bed. She had yet to sink into a cold, heartless world of complete bitchdom, so deciding to leave him sleep a while longer seemed more than caring, given their relationship. She quietly set down her packages making her way past the bed, into the bathroom.

While Angela showered, Jeff finally awoke to realize most of the day had slipped away. He was somewhat irritated with himself for not getting up sooner. Hearing the shower, he yelled in to her.

"Why did you let me sleep so long? There were some things I needed to do down in the kitchen offices before we went across the street for dinner." Then to himself more than directed at her, "Damn it."

Unfortunately for Jeff, Angela had finished bathing, was toweling off and had pushed the door open enough to hear his expletive. "For your information, Jeffrey, I figured you were only sleeping so hard and so long because your body needed the rest. So sorry for trying to be a considerate girlfriend, damn it."

They were about to start into it again. Angela decided she would nip it in the bud before wasting energy and emotion of her own on what seemed to be an increasingly lost cause.

"Things to do in the office? What about your father, Jeff? What about the fact that the man who loves you, raised you, and set you up with all you have today is lying in a hospital bed dying? Did you not tell me, and your mother for that fact, that you were definitely going by to see him today? What the hell is the matter with you?"

This was the first time since he had even mentioned visiting his dad that Jeff had thought about that promise. "Crap. Crap. Crap. I did want to go and see Pop." Looking at the clock, he realizes that cannot happen now. "I'll call my mother and have her hold the phone for him. A little pep talk will have to do for now. Let me know when you're done in there so I can get cleaned up as well."

She was close to being done but simply replied, "Fine."

Jeff grabbed the phone from the bedside table and noticed a missed call. His mom and dad's apartment number. Calling voice mail he replayed the message from his mother. Now he was really irritated at himself. At Angela. At anything and anyone for the most part. Clearly there was no time to get over to the hospital and check his father's status, he hit the button to call his mother back.

Straight to voice mail. "Mother, it's Jeffrey. Hey, I am so very sorry. Angela didn't wake me up and I pretty much slept most of the day away. I was hoping you could give me the what's up with Pop, but I guess you're still at the hospital. Anyway, we're going over to the Anderson's shortly. Give me a call as soon as you can and tell me how he's doing. I will definitely, definitely get by there tomorrow. For sure. Love you Mom."

Angela had only heard bits and pieces of the message he left due to the noise from her hair dryer. Sticking his head through the partially open door, he inquired as to her status.

"You mind if I jump into the shower? Need to get going. Thanks." He didn't really wait for her to respond, just entered, disrobed and pulled back the shower curtain. Water was warm still from Angela so he jumped right in without waiting for her approval.

Being the last to arrive to the closed Anderson restaurant, Jeff and Angela joined the other diners in the bar area for a pre-meal cocktail. Greg had even designed his very own signature drink for everyone to enjoy. He was, of course, in the kitchen working on the food, so the tardy couple helped themselves to a drink and moved about the room.

"Mr. and Mrs. Anderson, good evening. Thank you so much for inviting Jeff and me to your son's wonderful dinner party. I am so," she quickly corrected herself, "we, are so excited about experiencing Greg's culinary vision."

Jeff, still in a foul mood, knew enough to be cordial to his former best friend's parents. "Yes, thank you so much for having us. It has been quite some time since I've been over this way. Mr. Anderson, I must commend you on all you've done with your place, sir."

"Well, Jeffrey, all that praise must be redirected to my lovely Betty. All the interior designs, layouts, everything down to the silverware, glasses and plates are all of her choosing. I'll bet you never knew what a genius of a mother your friend had."

"Speaking of mothers, mine asked to regrettably send you her RSVP. You know Pop is not doing well, and things haven't gotten any better. She really felt her presence with him should take precedent to having fun here, at Greg's party."

Feeling a pang of guilt, Betty replied, "Oh, Jeffrey, you tell her no apologies are required. I feel terrible about not spending more time with her this week. I really wanted to go by and see your father as well, but with helping get things planned and organized, there was just never any time. I will be sure and call her first thing tomorrow morning. Gerry, you make sure we go and spend some time with Ray this week."

"As you wish, my dear. Thank you Jeff. You have all our love and condolences regarding your father. We can only keep him in our thoughts and hearts. Now the two of you go mingle and enjoy things. I believe dinner is to start any time now."

The dining room tables had been reset to accommodate 30 or so people. Betty had covered the edges of adjoining tables with large linens, creating the illusion of one very long, continuous table. Along with the settings, flowers and various furnishings, it all made for a spectacular presentation.

After his guests were seated, Greg appeared to a round of solid applause.

"Please, you might want to hold on to that until after dessert is served. You know you can't take it back, and if the food is bad, well, I don't want you to feel guilty for providing me with a false sense of security."

Laughter ensued and he continued, "This has been quite the journey for me, and I owe it all to my mother and father. Please, everyone share that warm applause for my folks, Gerald and Betty Anderson, without whom I would probably not be here. Nor any of you, for that matter."

The Anderson's were compelled to stand up and accept the crowd's appreciation. As the clapping subsided Greg finished. "Please sit back, relax and allow our amazing staff to serve you with the best I have to offer. Oh, pardon me for one more announcement. Course number 4 on your menu will not be served tonight. I was so looking forward to having my ingredients delivered first thing this morning so you would be able to enjoy the absolute most perfect dish. Unfortunately, the delivery never arrived. Those of you who cook for a living will understand how disheartening it can be not to have the ingredients you've envisioned. But, what can you do. Not to make excuses for them, but I was informed a bit ago that the delivery truck was involved in some sort of accident uptown which prevented them from getting here at all. Oh well. Everything else you see on the menu in front of you is good to go. We shall start immediately."

Food servers came out on cue and started placing the first course dishes in front of Greg's guests. He stayed long enough to share with the diners information about the food, wished them a good meal, and returned to the kitchen. Prior to leaving, however, he did gaze in Jeff's direction to determine if there was any immediate response to his food. Unfortunately, even though Greg had instructed his servers to make sure Angela and Jeff were among the first to receive food, there was nothing more than an absent, distracted look on Jeff's face. Greg could spend no more time there. He needed to get the next course plated.

The meal proceeded exactly as Greg had envisioned. He could imagine no other outcome as he had mentally prepared and served this dinner innumerable times in the previous few days. With every course served, Greg advised and delighted the diners with information and anecdotes about the dish. Prior to leaving the dining room each time he hoped to get some indication about how his food was presenting.

Just before leaving the dining room for the main course, he made his way to where Jeff and Angela were seated. "How are you two? Jeff it is great to see you, bud. Been a long time." He kept his voice down below the din of the room.

Angela answered him first. "Oh, Greg. Your food has been marvelous. We are both so proud of you."

Jeff was somewhat less enthusiastic. "Not bad, Greg. Nice meal so far."

"Is something wrong with your dinner, Jeff? Any advice on how I might make things better?"

Not wanting to be bothered, Jeff attempted to divert the request. "I'd really have to think about it. Give me some time and I'll get back to you, if you like."

"Absolutely, Jeff. Yes, anything you can do that will help sharpen my focus in creating great food would be much appreciated. Thanks, man."

Angela waited until their host was out of earshot. "Really, Jeffrey. You have to think about offering your friend some advice? Some friend you're turning out to be for him."

"I have way more important things on my mind than whether or not my former friend is a good cook. My father is dying, my restaurant is only slightly above average, my own food needs to get much, much better. I have a girlfriend who won't stop nagging the crap out of me about everything except what's important to me."

"So now Greg is your former friend? When did that happen?"

"Maybe the day he stepped on that plane to France? Maybe when he started writing letters to my girlfriend? Maybe when he just asked me to make him a better chef than I am. I don't know, Angela. I just know that I don't really have the time or energy to worry about Greg Anderson's career success."

"Don't throw those letters in my face. I've offered to let you read every word in every one of them. Nothing but a young man trying to repent for being an ass when we first met. Greg has been nothing but a true and sincere friend to me since he came back. You are really becoming quite the piece of work, Jeff. Quite the piece of work."

With everything on his mind, Jeff's impending explosion towards Angela was mercifully cut short as the servers started placing the main course plates in front of the diners. Angela only glared at him wondering more every second why she continued to stay with someone so completely self-absorbed.

"Now that you all have your main courses, I trust you'll find things to your satisfaction. Please everyone, bon apetit!" Greg circled the room ensuring his guests plates were the picture of perfection. It was difficult for him to understand where and when things went so wrong in his friendship with Jeff. Had he not gone to France, someone else would have. Besides, it was not Greg's fault that Jeff had been unable to go in the first place. Unsure where things were headed between the two of them he definitely did not like what he saw between Jeff and Angela. But what could he do? Attempt any sort of intervention and he would clearly show his true feelings towards her.

THE PERFECT MEAL

Even so, he desperately wanted her to be happy and in love with someone who loved her back, the way he knew he would if given the chance. He fought with his true feelings every day, every time he saw her. He would have to fight those feelings even longer. Unless Jeff figured out that he was losing Angela soon, Greg knew he might have a chance before long.

The food servers were taking away the main course plates when Jeff's pager vibrated; an unfamiliar number. He considered the call and decided it might have something to do with his restaurant. Leaning towards Angela, he spoke into her ear.

"I need to call these people back. It might be important. Work stuff."

At this point, Angela was rather disgusted with his presence and actually welcomed the chance to have him away from her. "Fine. Whatever, Jeff. I'm sure whomever is calling can not possibly wait another 30 minutes until we are finished here. Whatever."

Jeff got up and was forced to pass directly by Greg as the chef was about to reveal his meal ending masterpiece dessert. Somewhat confused and concerned about Jeff departing the table at this point, Greg inquired. His biggest fear was that something on the menu had made Jeff ill and he needed the restroom in order to recuperate.

"Everything okay, Jeff? You're not leaving, are you?"

"Just heading out to the lobby to return a call about work. I'll be back shortly."

"Well, you do not want to miss dessert. I'm hoping you really like what I've created."

Greg watched him leave, but had to refocus when one of the servers tripped and dropped a plate. While certainly not a travesty, the diners looked to Greg to see how he would respond.

"Well, I guess I won't be joining you in our final course. But that's okay, I got to lick the bowl." The waiter was busy cleaning up the mess when Jeff hurried back into the dining room. He got back to his seat, and without sitting down, whispered into Angela's ear.

Greg could see her face change from looking irritated to almost ashen gray. She placed her hand over her mouth in what he could only guess was shock. She leaned back towards Jeff with a reply but he was shaking his head. He turned and left the restaurant. No word to Greg or the other diners. He was gone.

20 ORPHANED IN AN INSTANT

He kept replaying the phone conversation over in his head. "This is Jeffrey Walker, someone called me from this number?" It was the hospital where his father was being treated so he knew whatever the news, it was unlikely to be good.

"Yes, Mr. Walker. You are the son of Ruth Walker?"

"I am. What's this about?"

"Mr. Walker, your mother was involved in an auto accident. She's currently in emergency surgery, sir. If you can, you should get here as soon as possible."

"She what? Car accident? Is she okay? Is she going to be okay? What exactly happened to her?"

The hospital representative sighed for what he knew was the coming frustration. "That is all the information I'm permitted to share with you over the phone, sir. My apologies, but it's our policy to only give details to family members in person, once we have verified their identification. Hopefully you understand, sir."

"UNDERSTAND?" he exploded into the phone. "My mother is in emergency surgery and you refuse to give me any idea at all what her current condition is? How understanding would you be if it was your mother in there?"

"I'd be very worried, obviously. The truth is, sir, I actually do not have any more information than what I've told you so far. They purposely keep us out of the loop so there is no temptation to break the rules of patient medical confidentiality. Sir, I can only advise you to come into the hospital's emergency surgery center as soon as you can. The admitting personnel will give you all the information they have at that time."

THE PERFECT MEAL

Jeff want to smash the phone against the wall. He refrained but still had the urge to shove a fist into through the drywall instead. He had to get out of Anderson's and get to his mother as soon as possible. Angela could tell him later about how wonderful Greg was and what a delight his dessert ended up being. He needed to leave and get to the hospital. It was all that mattered to him now.

Having made his way through his kitchens to the management office, he was unable to find the keys to the mini-van. They were normally hanging on hooks near the light switch, but they were gone. His frustration rising, it finally occurred to Jeff the message his mother had left about having taken the company vehicle.

"Fucking hell!" The employees were confused at their head chef cussing while passing through the kitchen to the stairs. He would have to grab his own keys and make his way to the parking structure down the block from his restaurant. He just couldn't grab 2 trains to get to the hospital in a timely manner.

Not that it was on his mind at the time, but Jeff had never made the journey from kitchen to apartment so quickly. Not even during the best of times with Angela and the allure of love making could entice him away from his culinary duties as fast.

Bursting through the front door of his place, he looked on the ledge which separated the kitchen from the living room area. He always placed his keys there after he had occasion to drive his car. They were not where he knew he had placed them.

"What the fuck? Where the hell are my god damned car keys? Fuck, FUCK, FUCK!"

Unknown to Jeff, Angela had attempted to reduce clutter and randomly placed items in the apartment. Since they had so few conversations of late, there had been no real chance to share with him that all of their keys were now on the labeled hanger just behind the front door. It was space that was otherwise unused and basically wasted, so she thought it would be great for one of those little message chalk boards that had brass key hooks.

Not seeing them anywhere, Jeff went into the kitchen to see if perhaps they might have fallen off the ledge and were stuck behind the roll away butcher block counter. Violently pulling it away from the half wall revealed nothing. Unfortunately the counter tipped over with the force and most of its contents went tumbling across the kitchen floor.

He could not be concerned with that right now. "What the hell did you do with my keys, Angela? Fuck." He spoke as if she were there in the room with him. "Maybe they're on the dresser?" He left the kitchen for the bedroom. Checking the the top of his chest of drawers revealed nothing in the way of car keys.

Now his anger was almost uncontrollable. He had to calm down if he were going to figure this out. Checking several drawers was useless as was looking on the counter where she put on her make up. Taking deep breaths to try and relax, he figured that a phone call to her was his only option.

It was as he headed back towards the kitchen the message board and key hooks caught his attention. Cleverly scribed in colored chalk was the word "KEYS".

"You're fucking kidding me," was all he said while grabbing the keys and bolting out the apartment. Taking the stairs three and four at a time was probably not the best choice. Jeff was lucky it was on that final jump to the ground floor that he had misjudged the distance and landed on the side of his foot. With his body moving at that speed, there was little doubt the snapping he heard and felt was going to be bad news.

On the floor near the foot of the stairs in immense agony, he laid for a moment to catch his breath and fight the tears he felt starting down his face. It took him a couple of minutes but he was eventually able to sit up and take stock of the throbbing, swelling appendage that was his ankle and foot. Pulling himself up to the second step, he had to take a break and breathe deeply in order to deal with the pain. It was then one of the line cooks appeared from the rear kitchen door towards one of the storage pantries.

He approached his boss who was sitting there in obvious pain. "Fucking hell, chef. What the hell happened to you?"

"Missed that damned last step. Might have broke my ankle. Get me a bag of ice and a large towel, will you?"

Jeff had to figure out how he was going to get to the hospital now. The cook returned handing the bag of ice to Jeff.

"The large towel is for your ankle chef. This smaller one is for the cut on the side of your head. Kind of bleeding down your face." He wiped at the abrasion while Jeff applied the ice and wrapped the towel around to hold it in place.

"I need you to take my car keys and run down the block to the parking garage. I'm in space 1516 on the 3rd floor. You can drive a stick shift, right?"

"Yes, chef."

"Look, my mother was in a car accident earlier and I have to get to the hospital. That's why I was in a hurry. Stick your head into the kitchen and yell for Jonny to come out here while you go get the car. Pull it up out back and I'll have him help me out. Go, now. Go!"

It took nearly 15 minutes before his car arrived at the back entrance of the restaurant. Jonny had helped Jeff out back, but couldn't stay with him since they were in the middle of dinner service. His pain was excruciating. Jeff didn't consider which direction his car would come down the alley and unfortunately for him, he was on the driver's side when it finally arrived.

THE PERFECT MEAL

He shouted at his employee when he pulled up. "Get out and help me to the passenger side, will you?" Jeff simply could not put any weight on his right foot at all. Nothing.

Finally into the seat, they sped down the alley and proceeded towards the hospital. This kid could drive pretty well, Jeff thought as he nursed his ankle, readjusting the ice bag so it would stay on the swollen areas.

"I know I told you to hurry, but my mother was already in an accident today, let's not make it a second Walker, okay?"

Before a reply came, Jeff simultaneously heard the siren and saw the rotating lights of the police car in the passenger side door mirror. "Fuck me. No fucking way. Are you kidding me. Unbelievable. Pull over quick, man. Maybe the dude will be cool and let us go so we can get to the hospital. Hell, maybe he'll even escort us."

Unfortunately that sort of thing only happened in movies and books. It most assuredly was not happening on that Sunday evening in Manhattan.

The more Jeff tried to explain why they were driving so fast the longer it seemed the officer took to write out the ticket. Finally giving up in frustration, Jeff decided he would follow up with this fellow's superiors. Even though the ticket was issued to the cook driving Jeff's vehicle, it was Jeff who was ultimately responsible. He made sure to tell his employee so.

"Don't worry, man. I'll make sure I pay for this ticket. I know you were only doing what I asked you. I'm really sorry." To the officer, as he ripped off the copy and handed it to the driver, "Sir, is your badge number and name on the ticket?"

It was, and with a smirk that told the occupants of the stopped car he would never be held accountable for doing his job, he turned and went back to his own vehicle. Jeff told the driver to go, they had to get to the hospital. "Just stay about 5 miles over the limit till we get there."

Nearly an hour had passed since Jeff had spoken with the hospital when they pulled up to the emergency exit. Finally at the admitting desk, the nurse leaned over the counter to assess Jeff's condition. Seeing him in a wheelchair she handed him a clipboard with blank forms and a pen. "Take these with you to the waiting area, sir. Fill them out, and we'll be with you as soon as we can."

More delays. "I don't need to fill anything out. I don't want medical care. I'm…"

She cut him off as she looked at his ankle wrapped with the towel and ice, "Sir, a sprained or broken ankle while certainly painful is not a big enough emergency to have you roll right in for treatment. Please go to the waiting room, fill out the forms I gave you and wait your turn."

He wanted to explode with pent up frustration but instead struggled up to his one good foot and looked down at the admitting person. He also paused, and took a deep breath calming himself so he could speak with confidence and poise.

"Miss, yes, I do have a messed up ankle. But that's not why I'm here. My mother was brought in this morning. She was in a car accident. Someone here called me to say she was in emergency surgery and that I needed to get her fast. Please, her name is Ruth Walker. Can you tell me where she is now and what's happening?"

People would try anything to get faster treatment in the emergency room, so his story did not immediately cause her to look things up. "I see sir. Can you please show me a picture ID? I need to verify you are who you say you are. What is your relation to Mrs. Walker?"

Another deep breath and sigh as he released it. "I am her son. She is my mother. Ruth Walker." Handing over his ID, "My name, as you can see right there, is Jeffrey Walker." With a final, soft plea, "Can you please tell me how my mother is doing. Please."

After a few keystrokes, the women looked back at Jeff. "There is nothing new to report, Mr. Walker. She is still in emergency surgery. If you'd like to go to the waiting room just outside the elevator on the 2nd floor? That is the best place to wait for news from the surgical team."

Still frustrated at having no new knowledge, he sunk back into his chair. "Thank you, miss."

Ever mindful of the restaurant, he told his cook to take the car and head back to work. "Thanks for the ride, and again, don't worry about that ticket. You let me know how much and I'll add it to your paycheck."

"Before or after taxes?"

"Get the hell out of here, will you. But seriously, thanks again for helping me out."

Taking the elevator up to the second floor waiting area, Jeff was reminded how much his ankle was throbbing. He winced when he bumped his foot while attempting to turn the wheelchair around elevator.

The doors opened, he noticed the waiting area straight ahead, double doors to the left with signs on each informing the reader that visitors were not allowed in that area of the hospital, staff only. To the right was a small desk area. There was no one on duty as he rolled towards it.

With the waiting area empty, Jeff figured the person who was supposed to be at the desk had found better things to do. "Hello?" Nothing. He looked around for one of those little service bells seen on the counter of a sleazy motel. Nothing.

"What the hell does a guy have to do to get some help around here?" Silence. He had been told this was where he needed to be, so he was reticent to go elsewhere in order to get more information about his mother. He decided to stay and wait until someone returned who could help him.

THE PERFECT MEAL

The 20 minutes which had passed might well have been hours. He had been rolling down towards the staff only doors, would turn the chair and roll back past the elevator, to the desk. He was about to turn in front of the desk when startled by the elevator doors opening. Finally, someone who looked like they worked here.

"Can you help me, please?"

"Sir, if you need your foot taken care of you should be down at the first floor emergency admitting area."

"No, miss. I was called. My mother was in an accident and they said she was still in surgery. That was like 6 hours ago. I'm here to find out what's happening. Can you PLEASE help me?"

"What's you mother's name sir?"

She looked up Ruth's current condition on the computer at the duty desk while Jeff looked on. He was in pain, concerned about his mother, and had not even considered what was happening with his father, Ray. He could only hope that the nurse would have good news for him.

"Mr. Walker, she is still in surgery. She's in pretty serious condition. I really do not know when there will be more news, but I'll make sure someone comes out as soon as they are able to let you know more. Please feel free to stay there in the waiting area. They could come out at any time with more information."

"Thank you." He was tired now, and just didn't have the energy to fight a losing cause. As he sat alone, waiting, his thoughts drifted back to dinner and Angela. He hated that he would have to apologize to Greg and explain everything which caused him to leave. Though frustrated with all of that, he figured it would be smart to call Angela and see if she could come. He was going to need a ride home when this was finally over.

Waiting for Angela to arrive, Jeff realized it had been nearly 7 hours they had been working on his mother. Finally, several medical technicians and what looked to be a couple of doctors came through the double doors. He did not need them to say his mother was in great condition, just that she was okay. She would pull through. Their faces expressed a different story.

"Mr. Walker?" One of the doctors stopped as the remainder of the group continued down past the desk, around the corner, out of sight. "Mr. Walker, you have my most sincere condolences. We did everything we possibly could to save your mother, but she was pretty banged up. She experienced some massive trauma to her head and torso during the collision with a food delivery truck. There was just too much damage. We couldn't get ahead of it. We were unable to save your mother, Mr. Walker. I am very sorry for your loss."

"She's … dead? My mother is, dead? Are you sure? She can't be dead, she just can't be."

"I am very sorry to be the one to have to tell you, sir, but I can assure you that Ruth Walker succumbed to injuries as a result of massive trauma. Again, I you have my condolences, sir." That was all the doctor reported to Jeff. He turned and followed the rest of his medical team and was soon out of sight. In that moment, Jeff realized the one thing he had forgotten. His father. He knew Angela would show up any moment but he could not wait. He had to get to his dad's bedside and make sure he could handle the news about the loss of his wife.

As fast as he could make the wheelchair go, he rolled to the elevator, pushing the up button. Once inside, he asked one of the passengers, "Could you push the 7th floor for me please. Thanks." This time he made the rotation of the wheelchair with caution. His ankle pain was as bad as it had been but he did not want it increasing due to his carelessness.

Since he was coming to see his father from a different direction, there was some confusion and disorientation when he got out of the elevator. He must have wheeled himself to the opposite end of the hospital floor before realizing his mistake. Frustrated, and anxious to get to his father, he turned the wheels with all his strength.

His father's room was just a few yards ahead. At this point, traveling at a fair clip, he realized stopping was an issue. He would have to grab the metal rim and try slowing down. On his initial attempt at this, he let go as both hands began to burn from friction. Instead he grabbed one of the wheel locks, yanking back on it.

Immediately stopping one wheel, the other continued to rotate. The chair lurched to the right ejecting Jeff. Being at the doorway to his father's room, he tumbled through, head first.

As he collected himself, he noticed a startled orderly in an otherwise empty room. "I'm sorry, I must be in the wrong place." The orderly was still trying to figure things out as Jeff sat up. "I'm looking for Mr. Walker. Raymond Walker? Do you know which room he is in? They must have moved him."

"Are you Mr. Walker's son, Jeff?"

"Yes, where is my father? Please I must get to him and tell him about Mom."

In his current emotional state and somewhat breathless from his wheelchair ordeal, Jeff had been on the floor, leaning against the wall with his back now to the doorway. He failed to notice when Angela arrived. She stood in silence. Jeff stared at this person who was cleaning and tidying up his father's former room.

"Mr. Walker passed away several hours ago. I believe the nurse called and spoke with your mother this morning, but I don't think she ever showed up to see him. You are the first family member to arrive." And then the patent line all the hospital employees seemed to have been trained to deliver. "I am so sorry for your loss, Mr. Walker."

Jeff was distraught. The orderly offered to help him up, but Jeff refused, remaining on the floor. He passed Angela on his way out, leaving her with more silent apologies. She bent down to try and console her boyfriend, but was only met with resistance on his part. He did not want to be touched.

Something occurred to Angela. With the passing of her father not too long ago, she had been finally orphaned after her mother passed so many years prior. In the span of just a few short hours, Jeffrey Walker, though a grown man, had been suddenly, and terribly, orphaned instantly.

21 TO THE BONE

Waking up and looking around, Jeff was uncertain where he was. The booze he had consumed after work with a bunch of brigade members must have been excessive. Slowly, he was able to determine someone must have deposited him in his folks apartment. He had not been here in the four months since they had died. The funeral was mostly a blurred memory. They held the wake at the restaurant, though he only remembered bits and pieces of the memorial. He recalled that Angela was the dutiful girlfriend, right up to the moment his alcohol consumption started to embarrass her.

It got very hazy after that. Had Greg helped his girlfriend take him to the apartment?

"I've got him Angela, you get the elevator. We should put him to bed and let him sleep it off."

On the ride up to the third floor she held one side while Greg supported most of Jeff's weight from the other. "This must be horrific for him to have to endure. Both parents on the same day? I thought the world had ended when my father passed away, Greg. But even then, we knew it was going to happen at some point soon."

"Apparently, Mr. Walker had taken a turn for the worse, but even then, I'm not sure Jeff was notified until the two of you found out. Pretty sure I'd be wasted off my ass too if I were in his shoes."

"You want my shoes, you can have them, Chef GG." Jeff attempted to kick off one of his dress loafers but failed. "You have no idea what it is to lose anything. You're a taker. A big, sneaky taker. Why don't you just take a hike?" His words were clearly motivated by deep seated frustration and booze paved the way for their delivery.

THE PERFECT MEAL

The elevator opened and they headed down the hall. Angela let Greg completely support her grieving, drunk boyfriend while she opened the apartment door. They made their way through to the bedroom.

"Thank you so much for helping get him home, Greg. He probably won't tell you, but you really are a good friend to him. To both of us." After tucking Jeff into bed, she walked back to the living room and gave her helper a big hug and kiss on the cheek.

Jeff was awake now and thinking a bit clearer. Sitting on the edge of the bed, moving very slowly he thought, "How long had she hugged him? And did they kiss? Why would she have kissed him? What a bastard Greg was for taking advantage of her that way."

He could have gone on like this for hours, and had several times over the past few months. Of course, that wouldn't help him now so he made his way into the shower and finished sobering up. It was late enough that Angela would have left for work. Thankfully, he would not have to deal with her for failing to come home last night.

In an effort to work out the cobwebs in his hung over brain, he walked up the stairs to get ready for work. Just as he hit the landing, Angela was exiting their apartment.

"Oh, hey. I thought you'd be off to work by now."

"I have that doctor's appointment. I told you about it yesterday. I guess you were too focused on work to notice."

"Sorry. I must have been."

"Where were you all night? I know you were drinking with the cooks after you shut down the kitchen."

"I guess one of them must have taken me to my folks place by mistake. I woke up there this morning but really don't remember how I got there. Didn't even realize I had their keys to get in. Sorry about that. It happens."

"It happens? Whatever, Jeff. I have to go before I'm late. We will talk about this later. Don't worry, I know where you'll be."

"No, let's talk about it now. You complain I never make time for you. I have time right now so let's get this over with. Come on."

"Sorry Chef Walker. You don't always get what you want. I told you I'm late. I'm leaving. Now!"

------ oOo ------

Dinner service that evening was particularly challenging for the kitchen. Mistakes were being sent out with little quality control. Most of that fell upon Jeff's shoulders, which only served to irritate him more as the evening wore on. One of the newer line cooks was consistent in his poor performance and Jeff was fed up.

"Have you ever worked in a professional kitchen before," the chef was yelling at the young cook. "My god, man. I've seen better knife cuts by a 10

113

year old little girl. Get your act together or get the hell out of my kitchen." He was hot and this target was as good as any for venting his anger.

"Yes Chef. Sorry Chef."

"Don't be sorry. Be right for fuck's sake."

"Yes Chef," the flailing cook replied.

"Final four top going out. Make it right people. I don't want to be here holding your hands all night long. Get your act together."

Picking up the plates, the server saw something missing from one of them. She was hesitant to point it out to the chef, but was more fearful of returning the plate once the customer had noticed.

"Chef Walker, not sure this looks right, sir. Will you check it out?"

If there were such things as straws breaking the camel's back, this was it. Jeff exploded on the line cook. "That's it, man. You're gone. Out. Get the hell out. Now. No, don't look around for help. They have all done their jobs and put the food on the plate. What have you done?"

"I, I don't know Chef."

"You don't know? Well I know. You fucked up immediately after I told you not to fuck up anymore. YOU FUCKED UP MAN. Jonny, finish up this plate pronto and get these people served. You, mister, fuck off. You can get out, and please, please, do not ever come back."

The poor kid was red in the face and shaking. He had always heard such great things about working for Chef Jeff Walker, but had never seen him like this. In his rush to get his personal tools packed up, he failed to see one knife which had lodged somehow between two prep stations, blade side up. The tool kit rolled up, he wiped his hands and tossed the towel blindly back towards his area. It landed covering the knife from view.

"Your check will be mailed to you tomorrow," Jeff shouted as the cook made his way out the back of the kitchen. To Jonny, "Rough service tonight. Where are we getting these so called cooks, Jonny? We've got to do better hiring, you know?"

"I know, I know, Chef. Here, have a belt." That was the first of several drinks over the next hour or so while the rest of the brigade cleaned up and shut things down.

By the time Angela showed up in the kitchen, Jeff was, yet again, intoxicated. Still drinking with Jonny and one other cook, he failed to notice as she stood by the dining room doors watching him down shots and bitching about his poor performance. Finally, she makes her presence known.

"Jeff, let's go up to the apartment. We need to talk about last night before you have a repeat performance."

His employees did not even make the case that she should join them for a few. These were definitely not the old days when it was nothing for Angela to have several drinks with her man and his cooks.

"Good night men. Same thing tomorrow? Do not stay up all night getting hammered. We need you tomorrow."

After they had left, he turned his irritation towards Angela. "What on earth would possess you to act like that in front of my employees? You cannot do that to me. It undermines my fucking authority around here."

"I'm sorry, but you're drinking way too much night after night. It's not doing either of us any good."

"I'm not drinking to do you good, Angela. We had a shitty dinner service, I was forced to fire a line cook, and this was the best way to try and let it go."

"That doesn't matter, Jeff. You can't get drunk every night in front of your employees either. How do you think that affects your authority?"

"It's part of the job. You would know that if you'd ever spend any time down here with me. You were probably over at Anderson's getting cozy with Chef GG, weren't you?"

He was about to push her too far. "You're so wrong, Jeffrey. Why would you say that about me and Greg. You know we are just friends. He's your friend too, you know."

"Well, I'm certainly not his friend. You know he's just trying to take you from me. Steal you away like he's done with all my other dreams."

She knew they were nearing the end of their relationship, but certainly hoped to have better memories of its ending. Trying yet again to calm herself, she approached him with arms extended.

"Look, I'm sorry you had such a crappy day. I get it. You're upset and we didn't start things off very well this morning. Why don't you put down the drink and let's go upstairs and figure this all out."

"I don't want to put down the drink and go upstairs. I certainly do not want to spend the rest of the evening figuring things out. Again. For the thousandth time. Why don't you just go away and leave me alone?"

With far less malice intended than his drunken actions produced, Jeff shoved her away so that she could not embrace him. Being much bigger than she, his power caught her off guard and she stumbled back towards the line cooks' work stations.

Catching a heel on one of the rubber floor mats, she continued falling towards the table's surface. Mostly by instinct her right arm moved backwards in the direction of the fall. She should be able to right herself on the table top with support from her forearm. Unknown to her, the towel she was only inches away from was harboring a very painful secret.

22 FALL AND RISE

Jeff was too drunk to be of any help at this point. Angela's arm was deeply lacerated and she thought she could see bone at one point. She found a stack of clean kitchen towels on the shelf above the work station. Wrapping several around the cut she tried to stop the bleeding. Though inebriated, the sight of that much blood forced Jeff to realize he had made a mistake.

"I'm sorry Angela. I am so sorry. Please forgive me. I didn't mean for that to happen. I really did not mean to hurt you. Are you okay? Shit, shit, shit. Come on, let's go to the hospital. I'll get the car."

She was not surprised that he would think himself capable of driving her through Manhattan traffic in his current state. "Are you out of your mind? There's no way in hell I would let you drive me to the next block much less to the hospital. You are drunk, Jeff. You just shoved me into a knife which nearly cut my arm off. You think I'd go anywhere with you? Leave me alone. I'm calling Greg."

Not the thing Jeff needed to hear at that moment. He had clearly messed things up. Bad. He could only sit there and watch while she kept pressure on the towels in an effort to stop the bleeding and dial the kitchen phone at the same time.

"At least let me help you dial the phone. Pretty sure I can handle that without endangering your life."

"No. I can do it. I do not want your help. Get away from me." Somehow, she was able to get Greg's number dialed. By the time they found him and he spoke to her, Jeff had taken his bottle and stumbled towards the elevator.

"Hey Angela. Was just thinking about you as we finished up around here. What's up?"

THE PERFECT MEAL

"Greg, I need your help. Can you get your car and pick me up out front? Please?"

She didn't need to say please nor ask him twice. "I'll be there in seven minutes." He was there in under five. Angela never asked for help from him, at least not with that tone of voice. He knew it was serious and was certainly not prepared when he saw her clutching blood soaked towels around her arm as he pulled in front of Walker's restaurant.

"What the hell?" he was shouting towards her while popping out of the driver's side to open her door and help her into the car. "What happened to you? What happened?"

She was a little light headed, but not so much that she was unable to tell Greg the details of her argument with Jeff.

"What? He cut you? HE CUT YOU?"

"It wasn't like that, Greg. It was an accident. Really, it was. Can you just get me to the emergency room so they can stitch this up? It sort of hurts, you know?"

So many thoughts were racing through Greg's head as he drove through the sparse, evening traffic.

"We'll get you there, don't worry. Try to hold that arm up if you can. Lean it against the window." In an attempt to inject a bit of levity into the otherwise serious situation, "Oh, try not to bleed all over my car, will you? I just got it detailed." He smiled at her.

She attempted to smile back while raising her arm, but pain wiped her face with a grimace instead. "This old heap? This is what you call having it detailed? I don't know, Greg. I think a little blood red color might actually add some value to what you're calling a car."

It was the most she could offer in retort. He laughed and proceeded to get get his friend the medical attention she needed. Angela was happy Greg stayed with her at the emergency room. She was frustrated at the interactions with Jeff, but more sad than anything else. By 3:30 am, the two were again in the car and driving home.

"You're not going to go back to your apartment, are you?"

She had not thought about it until that moment. "Oh, you're right. I can't be there right now. I guess I could stay at a hotel or something. I need to figure out what I'm going to do next."

"You're not going to any hotel, at least not right now. You can have my bed, and I'll sleep on the couch. I do that half the time anyway, so it's not like I'll be put out or anything. Tomorrow, after you wake up you can figure things out."

"Oh, Greg. Are you sure? I would be so grateful to not have to think about anything right now. Besides, the pain meds they gave me are really kicking in. I might sleep until the day after tomorrow."

"Of course, I'm sure. When we get up to my apartment, why don't you call and leave a message at your office telling them you won't be in? That way you can sleep without worrying about your work responsibilities."

"Good idea, I will." He was pulling into his parking spot in the alley behind the restaurant. Just one of the perks of being the head chef there. He helped Angela out of the car, and upstairs. She left Shelly, her office manager the message, and with Greg's help was able to navigate into his bedroom.

Kissing him on the cheek, she wanted to express her gratitude. "Thank you so much, Greg. I truly don't know what I would have done without your help."

"No need to thank me, again. We're friends. That's what friends do. They are there for each other through thick and thin. And bloody arms and things. Now you get some rest. I put a glass of water on the night stand, and more of your meds in case you need them. Go to sleep. I'll see you when you wake up."

That was the last thing Angela remembered hearing as she drifted off. She could worry about what came next tomorrow when her wits were more about her.

------ oOo ------

Thinking he was in a world of hurt because of the hangover was the least of the pain Jeff would be feeling before long. This time, he had come to his parent's apartment on his own. Last night's events were coming back. Shame and embarrassment were at the forefront of the incoming emotional wave.

"I've really done it this time," he spoke to the pictures of his mother and father on their bedroom walls. "Where are you guys when I need you? Mother, I know you would have the right things to tell me round about now. Pop, if you were here, you'd tell me I was screwing up everything in my life. And I'd tell you I know I am. I am, but I can't help it. I really can't."

Their photos only smiled in silent reply. Jeff got up, grabbed his dirty chef jacket, and headed a floor up to get ready for his day in the kitchen. Once in his place, he placed the jacket on the coat rack with several others needing laundered. He took a shower, all the while simultaneously regretting his actions from last night and the effects they likely would have on his relationship with Angela.

He knew it was over between them, and that was too bad but at least there would be more time for his food, and getting things back in proper order with his career. At this point, he felt the best thing would be to put his head down, and find that magic again as he pursued the only culinary goal that meant anything to him.

------ oOo ------

Once back in the kitchen, Jeff was able to get into meal prep flow, and block everything else out. About an hour into the lunch service, Angela's face appeared in the window of the door between the kitchen and dining room. Looking up at that moment, Jeff motioned for her to come through. They needed to talk, and though he was busy, he would make the time. This time.

"How are you?" He could see her bandaged arm and was not very proud of his part in the accident. "Are you doing okay? I am so sorry about last night. You know I didn't mean for that to happen. That knife belonged to the guy I fired yesterday. Typical of him to leave that little unsuspecting treat for the rest of us."

She thought, "No, typical of you to push the blame away from yourself." She said to him, "I know you didn't mean for me to nearly cut off my arm, Jeff. Don't worry about it. They sewed me up and gave me pain meds. I'm doing fine."

"Listen, I know we need to talk about things. Will you be around in a few hours? I'll come up after we finish lunch."

"I'll be upstairs, but please don't come up. I'm packing my things and moving out. We are through, Jeffrey. I know this particular incident was not done with malice on your part, but we both know things have been wrong with us for a long time. You need your space to deal with your grief. I've felt consistently second place in your life for most of the time we've been together."

"That's not true, Angela. That's not really how it is with me."

"Yes, that's how it really is with you. And it's okay. I want the best for you, Jeff Walker. Only, I wanted to be a bigger part of what was best in your life. If we're honest with ourselves, you know that your food, your perfect meals are the only thing which matters to you. I'm okay with that. Now."

"But," he stops himself because he knows what she says is the truth. Looking into her eyes he opens up for the first time in quite a while. "Where will you go? I know things are still pretty tight with your business. Look, I can stay downstairs in my parents old place so you don't have to rush out of here. I don't mind."

"That's considerate of you, but I think I would be uncomfortable staying in our apartment any longer than I need to. I don't have much stuff, just my clothes and a few odds and ends. If you'll just give me the afternoon and evening, I'll be out of there and out of your hair."

"So you already have a place to go? That was fast."

"It really shouldn't matter, but yes, I do. And yes things are pretty tight, financially, with my business. Greg's parents were kind enough to offer me one of their available apartments for a reduced rate, just until my cash flow picks up a bit. I am very grateful to them for caring about me so much." She could see on Jeff's face that her announcement was not going to sit well with him. "Please. Just keep your thoughts and comments to yourself. At this point, I don't need to hear what you think you need to say. It just no longer matters Jeff. Really, it doesn't."

She left him in the kitchen to start packing her stuff for the move across the street. For the first time in her life, she would have space all to herself. There was a short period after her father had passed when she lived in their apartment alone, but most of that time was spent grieving. There had no appreciation of the freedom.

Then she had met Jeff and moved in with him. Their future was so bright and promising. It even delivered on that potential at first, but then his review, and subsequent culinary pursuits. That is where she would point a finger at the beginning of their end.

Once upstairs, she found some flattened cardboard boxes under the bed and started taping them together. Almost immediately, she saw the antique meat thermometer sticking out of the pocket of Jeff's dirty jacket. Even though sunlight was streaming through a nearby window, the gauge was dull, the decorative jewel on its face without a sparkle.

Finding the original wooden container Greg had sent the gauge in, she gently laid the thermometer into its silk lined space, closed the lid, and placed it at the bottom of the first box.

At precisely the same moment, downstairs in the Walker's restaurant kitchen, a bright reflection of light from his sous chef's knife caught Jeff's attention. It only took that brief distraction for most of his fingernail and the tip of his digit to be severed from his non-knife holding hand.

THE PERFECT MEAL

23 ANGELA'S REALIZATION

1992 was just around the corner. In the three months since Angela had left, Jeff had found it increasingly difficult to function well in his kitchen. For the first few weeks after their break up, the pain in his cut off finger was the constant reminder of the pain he wanted to feel in his heart. Knowing he was wrong and feeling it were two different things.

As much as he wanted to blame her for some portion of their challenges, it was hard to find the intellectual justification. Because of his knife injury, several days had passed before being able to get back to cooking. As a result, there had been no need to use a meat thermometer. Sometime after she had moved out, Jeff realized Angela had taken back the antique gauge. He would dwell on that single fact until finally recognizing it had only ever been a loan for the one they had broken during their love making.

Making love in the afternoon. That was something he missed. In the meantime, they had just received another less than stellar review. Things had to change for him and the restaurant. Much more of this bad press and he might find himself out of business.

At the beginning of December, the night of the first major snowstorm to hit their area, Jeff took the evening off. The weather had kept most of their customers away from dinner. Better that than them not coming because some fickle food writer dissatisfied with how his steak had been cooked.

Sitting in his living room that evening, drinking alone, as he tended to do, he pondered his fortune of late. Not having been raised religious or overly superstitious, he wondered whether all of his culinary luck had left his life with Angela's departure.

While clearing out his parent's things and getting their apartment ready to rent, he set aside framed photos of his mom and dad in individual shots as well as several of them both; many in loving embraces with sincere affection washing across their faces.

As Jeff sat there on that cold, snowy night, he spoke to his folks. "Things are really spiraling out of control. As you know, Angela has left. Can you believe she's living across the street above Anderson's?"

"Yes, I know I've told you that before."

"Yes, many times. I know."

"Anyway, we just got yet another bad write up. I think she took all of my good fortune with her."

"What?"

"I know we don't believe in that sort of thing. But then you had me believing as a kid that I had the ability to grow a new arm if anything should ever happen to one of mine. Well, guess what?"

He held up his healed, but still pinkish, stump of a left index finger. "Guess that was a bunch of superstitious hogwash as well. No regeneration happening here, folks."

Nothing in return from the pictures. There never was. He poured himself another. Sat alone in silence. Tomorrow he would turn things around. Tomorrow's food would be perfect, every bit of it. Slipping into unconsciousness, that old cliche slogged through his brain, "Tomorrow is always a day away."

In those same months since their break up, Angela had made quite the cozy home for herself. Business was picking up for her, allowing her to pay market rate for the apartment. She was even exploring the world of furnishings. Coming home from work she experienced her own peaceful sanctuary, protection and tranquility. As a bonus she was getting a work out now that she lived on the 4th floor taking the stairs most of the time.

It was also very convenient having Greg nearby. The first few months it seemed like they spent most evenings together after he left the kitchen to be cleaned up by his staff.

"Greg, how come you are able to spend so much time with me and not seem to have a challenge with the fact that your people are working downstairs? Jeff was never able to do that. I rarely saw him before 11 or 12 every night."

"My dad had a saying when I was growing up. Whenever I didn't really want to do something, he was right there telling me, 'In the end, you'll do what you want to do.' It took me a long time to figure out what that one meant."

"Basically, whatever we end up doing we did it because that's what we really wanted to do the most?"

"Bingo, Skippy. At least that's my take."

THE PERFECT MEAL

It was conversations like that one which she held onto and had helped her begin to heal from the breakup. Every day she was more grateful for Greg's friendship.

Perhaps 6 weeks after the move, Angela started noticing something interesting during her time with Greg. He had always been attentive. Much more than the attention she had ever gotten during her relationship with Jeff But lately it seemed that he would sit a little closer to her when they hung out. Holding the elevator had always been one of his gentlemanly acts, but when had he started holding her hand and placing his other on the small of her back as he guided her into or out of it?

She was probably imagining these things until a couple of weeks ago when they had watched a chick flick. Angela never realized how sensitive a guy her friend was.

"Are you crying? Are you crying? You are, you're crying! Oh my goodness. I cannot believe you are such a cry baby. I'm sorry, Greg. We won't watch any more tear jerkers. I promise."

Of course she was just poking fun at him, and as was their usual schtick, he countered with, "Uhm, excuse me miss. But are them great big alligator tears streaming down your face I see?"

Reaching to feel her cheek, Angela wiped at the tears she knew already to be there. "Am not. I'm not crying. I'm not a big, sensitive cry baby."

They both laughed so hard that eventually her head was on his shoulder, which she punched with abandon several times during their fit of emotion. Remembering back she recalled holding Greg's hand for quite some time.

Now the first of December and road conditions were quite challenging for her drivers due to the first snow of the season. About mid-way through the afternoon, she sent message by radio to each driver to call the day off and head back to the offices. Better to be safe than have someone get in an accident and put themselves or her vehicles out of commission. The streets department would have things cleared up by tomorrow. Her customers would surely understand.

Getting home at a reasonable hour, she popped into the restaurant to see how busy they were given the weather. Several of the employees were in the lounge and greeted her with a unified cheer. Since Greg had taken over and his father had taken to traveling the world with his mother and little sister, the staff had finally gelled into a tight unit. In the nearly 3 months she had been living above the restaurant, she had gotten to know many of them during the late night revelries.

Entering the lounge, she saw Greg sitting with some wait staff at the bar. As she approached everyone surrounding the chef got up moved to a table, giving them privacy.

"Hey, where's everyone going?" Angela pleaded. "Don't leave on my account. Greg, make them come back."

"Why? I made them go away. I wanted to hang out with my friend. Alone. Is that so wrong? Sue me."

"I just may, Gregory Anderson. I may if I don't get a glass of wine in the very near future."

Greg beckoned the bartender who inquired, "What shall it be tonight, my lady?"

"Wine. Red. Pinot. Unopened bottle. Please."

How could Greg tell this woman, this goddess in his eyes, no? "Bar keep. Make it so."

The bartender set up two clean glasses, uncorked the bottle, poured them each a serving, then left them alone. During that first glass she noticed they were sitting extremely close together. Closer than just normal friends might consider comfortable. But she was comfortable.

"Excuse me sir, but isn't your chair a little too close to mine? The only way you might be nearer to me would be if you were sitting on my lap." The look on Greg's face told her he was seriously considering that possibility. "Oh, no you don't, buddy."

"No? Well phooey. Oh, wait, what's that?" He cupped a hand around his ear as if straining to hear some distant voice. "Yes, Mother. Yes. Right away Mother. Leaving right now, Mother." Then, back to her in that fun, smart ass way of his, "Sorry, I have to go. My mommy is calling me." He began to get off his bar stool.

She grabbed, jerking him back onto the chair and as a consequence ended up pulling the seats so close they now touched. "Oh no you don't, mister momma's boy. You're not getting away. We just started this bottle of wine, and I am not finishing it alone."

"Very good point. I am pretty sure I'm paying for that wine. Just so you know, I'm only staying to get my money's worth."

"Is that so? That's the absolute, only reason you are staying and hanging out with me?" Without notice, without so much as the first indication, Angela sat up straight, reached one hand around his neck, and pulled his head down. As their lips were about to touch, "Perhaps this might entice you to stay?"

The moment he had been waiting for had finally arrived. She was about to kiss him after all these years. Unable to move, not due to fear of the contact, but because every dream he had ever had about her always started with the two of them passionately embracing. They always ended with the sun rising and her snuggling close to him under the covers.

Only half way into their second glass of wine, she mistook his hesitation. Pulling away from the embrace she was convinced of her mistake and looked away as she started apologizing.

"Oh. Oh, my. Greg. Oh, I am so sorry. I mean, I didn't think. I can't even blame the wine. We haven't had that much to drink. Please forgive me. I didn't mean to. I'm such an idiot. Will you please forgive me?"

He was now laughing softly at her while thinking, "Note to self. Stop thinking so much. Start acting." He returned her question. "Forgive you for what? For being such a tease? You act like you're going to kiss me and then you freak out as if you're about to engage in a Deadly Sin? Forgive that? I don't think so, Ms. Harris."

There was no thinking, and not an ounce of hesitation when Greg cupped Angela's face with his two strong hands and pulled her close. He pressed his lips into hers for what seemed about 3 hours.

In reality the kiss was nowhere near that long, but Angela was captivated by the embrace just the same. She had pondered about the little things happening between them recently, but work and life and everything prevented her from adding it up. That kiss, however, had certainly solved the equation.

There was silence between them. Not the uncomfortable, who should say what next silence one might expect after an unsavory act. Instead, they drunk in the beauty which surrounded them without feeling the need to find the words.

Finally, Greg reached up and emptied the bottle into their glasses. "Another?"

"Another, kind sir."

So went the next couple of hours. A bit of wine. A little conversation. Some kissing. As they reached their fill of wine the conversation increased. As did the kissing. Neither participant had been watching the clock but after some time, and most of the employees having exited the building, the bartender spoke up.

"Uhm, boss? I'm all done here. I could stay, but there's really nothing left for me to wipe down or set up for lunch tomorrow. You two good? Should I leave now?"

Looking around, taking stock of their environment, Angela shyly covering her nose and mouth with her napkin, spoke to Greg. "Oh, my Mr. Anderson. What has happened here? Did you make them all go away so we could be alone? Bad boy, Mr. Anderson."

"That will be all barkeep. You are hereby dismissed. You saw nothing here tonight. Nothing happened here tonight. You shall go away and wonder why the evening was such a bore." His smiling wink told the bartender everything.

"Yes sir, boss, chef, sir. Nothing to see here. Good night boss. Good night Ms. Was Not Here All Night With the Boss."

She moved the napkin down away from her mouth just far enough to extend her tongue towards the exiting bartender. Laughing, Greg gently placed his hand on hers and guided it back up to cover her open mouth.

"Don't bite yourself, Ms. Harris. You're only just healing from that nasty arm cut. Of course, if you do bite your tongue, you probably wouldn't be able to talk very much for a few weeks. Hmmm…"

"I also wouldn't be able to do this." She stood on the rungs of her stool and was now slightly taller than he was sitting down. Looking down at him, she planted what must have been the thousandth kiss on him that evening. Leaning into him, her stool started to slide away. This left her straddling one of his thighs.

"Oh. Oh, my," she uttered as soon as they stopped long enough to take a breath. Obviously that position was conducive to escalating their sexual arousal, especially hers. Sliding down his thigh, ever so slowly, until she had her feet on the ground, she stood up straight.

"Well, Mr. Anderson. I do believe we should throw ourselves out of this establishment." They had finished two and a half bottles of very nice pinot noir, and subsequently were a little heady. The sexual tension between them was a very strong attraction at that point. "I happen to live near by. Could I interest you in a cup of very strong coffee?"

"Coffee, you say? Coffee? As in come up to my place for a cup of coffee, coffee? I, my dear would love a cup of your very strong coffee."

They left the bar, rode the elevator up to Angela's apartment. Reaching her front door she remembered, "Oh, I'm very sorry Mr. Anderson, but I ran out of coffee just this morning. I have no very strong coffee to offer you."

"In that case, Ms. Harris, I shall bid you farewell."

Angela would have none of his trying to escape her clutches. Greg did not try hard to leave, either.

Once inside, she made excuses for not wanting to move things off the couch for them to sit down. Instead, she took Greg by the hand and led him into her bedroom. He knew where this was going, and thought better about letting it get there.

"Excuse me, miss. Just what do you think you are doing?" He pulled away from her grasp.

With a fabricated sad expression like someone had stolen her puppy she chided him. "What's the matter? You getting chicken feet, Mr. Anderson?"

Between the look on her face and her quip, he started laughing. She had backed her way into the bedroom and was extremely seductive in the unbuttoning of her blouse. Mesmerized by her beauty and seduction he was incapable of doing anything but following.

Kicking off shoes, she jumped onto the bed landing upright, but on her knees. As he approached, she sat with her feet out to the side of her thighs.

THE PERFECT MEAL

The closer Greg got, the further she leaned away until he was upon her, she flat on her back. For the briefest moment, he considered how limber she was to be able to hold that position.

But she did not hold it for very long. As they continued to embrace, she somehow unbent her legs without moving from the prone position and slid them around his midsection. Always wondering what this might be like, he was living it here and now.

For several more minutes they grappled in ecstasy. Then, without a word, Angela pulled away from him, unbuttoned her pant waist, and slowly, ever so slowly removed each pant leg.

"You could blind a normal man with a stunt like that, Ms. Harris. Whatever do you think you are doing? Is that some new fangled way of making coffee?"

"No, sir. The only thing this has to do with making coffee is they are both hot. And it's a very good thing you are not a normal man. Imagine how hard it would be for you to continue in your culinary career if you were blind. Now, kind sir, would you close that door, remove your clothes and find yourself in bed next to me, please."

There was very little use in fighting her powers. Reaching back to close the door, he proceeded to do as he was told.

23 THE PERFECT MEAL

Even with heavy curtains covering her bedroom windows, Angela was awakened by bright slivers of sunlight. With so much snow from the night before, everything out side was ultra white and the sun's reflection magnified the illumination inside her apartment.

In bed, a decent sized hang over had her moving slow and deliberate. Then she remembered.

"Well, gosh darn it, Greg Anderson. Where did you go?"

She knew they had messed around a bit but her memory was hazy after the point she had gotten under the covers.

"Oh my gosh. Please tell me I remember being with him?" Her synapses might as well have been firing in molasses. She had no recollection of what might have happened.

"Did he...did I..." Nothing. No recall.

Rolling onto her stomach she noticed her shoes had been placed neatly beneath the chair next to her dresser. The clothes she had been wearing yesterday were neatly folded on the seat. Her sweater evenly hung on the back of the chair.

"Did I do all that? Don't think so. Even on my best days, I never put my shoes there." Then it occurs to her. Greg must have done this. He must have tidied up her things before he left her room last night.

"I bet nothing at all happened once we were in bed." While this made her a bit sad, she also had immense respect for him.

Savoring those thoughts she glanced to the lower shelf of her bedside table. On it was a paperboard box containing all the letters Greg had sent her during his time in France. It had been forever since she had thought about them. Grabbing the box she started flipping through the envelopes.

THE PERFECT MEAL

Sitting up in bed, Angela read. This time what was between the lines. The first few were filled with apology and remorse at how he was when they first met. From there his letters related some of the interesting things he had seen or done while at school in Paris. Even after he had sent her the antique thermometer, the tone of his letters was warm, friendly. Not a single time had he crossed that arbitrary line between being friends and asking for something more.

Yet, there was an undertone amidst the words on the page, one she had failed to pick up on during her first reading of his letters.

"Well Greg Anderson. I do believe you love me. In fact, I believe you have loved me since you sent me that meat thermometer." With what amounted to a school girl giggle, she leaned over the edge of the bed and looked for the wooden box. Several minutes had passed since she awoke, and a bright shaft of sunlight was now streaming directly onto her lap. Almost as if it had been scripted, she had a spotlight focused on the meat thermometer when the box lid was opened.

After a few more moments of contemplation, Angela closed the box, threw back the covers, and bounced out of bed. Airmail letters which had been resting on the bedspread went flying in all directions. She held tight to the thermometer until setting it on the dresser when she dressed in jeans and a sweater. Slipping into sneakers and a quick brush of her hair was all she needed.

Grabbing the box, she left her apartment and ran down the stairs towards Anderson's kitchen. Surprised at how quiet it was just an hour and a half before lunch, she was a little confused.

"What's happening? Was the time wrong on my clock?" She called out, louder, "Hello? Anyone home?"

A young man with dark hair covered by a net stuck his head around the corner from the dish room, "Hola? Oh, hello Ms. Harris. How are you today?"

"Truth be told, just a little groggy from last night, but don't tell. Hey, do you know where everyone is? I was hoping to talk to Greg."

"Oh, si. We are just about to have lunch and chef asked me to come get some extra plates to share some of the new dishes he's prepared today. Come. We'll go out together."

"So kind," she thought as they left for the dining room. Handing his chef the plateware, the dishwasher also nodded for Greg to notice who was following him out.

"Well, good morning, sleeping beauty. Everyone, say hello to Ms. Was Not Here All Night Drinking Wine With the Boss."

Angela looked at him. Then she stared at the bartender who apparently told everyone she indeed had been there all night drinking with their boss.

The staff burst out laughing while offering hearty morning greetings. Her only reply was to stick her tongue out in their general direction, which did not last long because keeping herself from joining them in the good cheer was more control than she could exert.

"So, there you have our lunch menu people," Greg was finishing up. "Make sure you really take the time to taste each dish. Savor it and get a real feel for how you'll describe it to your customers. These people pay good money and want you to tell them exactly what they're ordering. I'm going to go chat with Ms., well Ms. you know who." He pointed in Angela's direction. "But I'll be back to test your ability to describe this food. Above all, people, enjoy your lunch."

A round of applause and several "thank you, chef" comments followed Greg and Angela as they walked towards the front doors.

"Hey you. I trust the gang didn't embarrass you too much? That darned bartender was already spreading news of our late night when I got to the kitchens this morning."

"No, of course not. But I showed them who was boss, don't you think?"

"Oh, absolutely you did. How'd you sleep?"

"Honestly don't remember much after getting into the bed."

Greg couldn't resist. "You don't remember after we went to bed? Wow. Thanks a lot. I guess I know where I rank in that department."

She couldn't resist either. "Sorry fella. You've either got the right stuff or you don't." Then she punched him in the arm. Hard. "Oh, stop it. You went home like you had little chicken feet, didn't you?"

"I went home because the gorgeous woman that I cared so much about passed out as soon as her head hit the pillow. I suppose I could have stayed. And done things."

That earned him another punch. "I know we didn't do anything, silly. But what is this about a woman you cared about? You don't care for her anymore?"

"Chef, someone on the phone wanting to talk to you about supplies or something." They were interrupted by a staff member.

To Angela, "Oh, hold on a second." To the waiter, "I'll take it at the hostess stand."

She faked a pout for his amusement, turning toward the door she looked back at him and said, "I'm leaving, Greg Anderson!"

In the few seconds it took her to get out the door, Greg sprinted to pick up the phone. Not waiting to even hear who was on the other end, "Hey, Chef Anderson here. Listen, kitchen emergency. Grease fire. Call me back in about an hour."

He hung up and was out the door before it had closed behind Angela. He was moving so fast that the force of his passing the door caused it to latch open.

Not making it far, not that she was trying, she continued to play hurt, keeping her back turned to him.

"Aw, come on now, little miss. Did someone get their feelers hurt?" He reached for her with both hands and spun her around. They were now facing each other, standing in front of the open restaurant.

"Yes. Someone's feelers are all bent up. And someone thinks someone else needs to fix this situation. Right now."

Again, he was immediately under her spell and did as she commanded. Bending down he locked his arms around hers, picked her up and proceeded to kiss away those bent feelers of hers.

"Put me down, Mr. Anderson. I have something to give you."

Gently lowering her back to the ground and releasing his bear hug, he now noticed that she was carrying a familiar looking object. It only took a moment, and he remembered back to that afternoon in France when he had found the quirky antique.

"Do you know what is inside this box, sir?"

"A new car?"

"Well, you do need a new car, but the only model that would fit in here would be of the matchbox variety. No silly. You know what it is, don't you?"

She slowly opened the lid as she asked the question she knew the answer to.

"Ta da!"

"Of course, I remember this. It was my friendship gift to you back when you hated me."

"Oh, Greg, I never hated you. I didn't like you very much, but never hated you. How could I? You were so sweet in all your letters. When I woke up this morning and you weren't there I re-read some of them. You know what I saw?"

"Poor penmanship on cheap airmail paper?"

Slug in the arm. "Well, yes definitely saw that. But beyond that?" She didn't wait for his response. "I felt the warmth and sincerity of a man who had been trying to tell me how he felt, deep in his heart."

"Wow. So you were getting love letters from someone besides me? Now I'm really jealous."

He would have to stop. His arm was getting quite sore.

"Ah hah! You admit that you were indeed sending me love letters, then? I knew it. I knew you wanted to be more than just friends."

"And just when do you think you knew this?"

She had been caught. Her response was to do the pouting lip thing. "This morning, after waking up all alone and reading your letters again. And that's when I saw the thermometer and decided that you should have it back. Not because I don't love it, but because I do."

Opening the box, she pulled the gauge out and handed it to Greg. He placed his hand around the long, metal stem, she laid a hand around his. With her other hand she reached for his neck pulling his ear close to her lips.

"Thank you, Gregory Anderson, for loving me as you have all these years. What you've shared makes me more grateful than you could ever know. My only wish is to share with you how that love has enveloped my heart and soul."

"I do love you, Angela Harris. Completely and unconditionally."

As they kissed, two subtle, yet extremely interesting events occurred simultaneously. Because the front door of the restaurant had remained open, the low level of sound from the staff made its way to their ears. Not until the moment when Angela expressed her thanks and devotion to Greg had they really been able to make out the words being spoken.

"The chef's new dishes are amazing."

"Where on earth did all this talent come from all of a sudden?"

"This has to be the perfect meal!"

They could hear the comments but were still somewhat preoccupied.

The second event had to do with the slightly brighter than one would imagine reflection of the snow enhanced sunlight bouncing off the face of the old meat thermometer still held in the lover's hands.

It was that light which had reflected directly into the eyes of an observer across the street while he drank a lukewarm cup of particularly bitter coffee.

From the moment Angela burst through Anderson's front door with Greg close behind, until being blinded by their light, Jeffrey Walker sat in silence and watched.

EPILOGUE

He knew all was lost where Angela Harris was concerned. Though unlikely they had put the show on for him, it was clear what the message of their performance meant. They had left the sidewalk now, arms wrapped around waists. Disappeared back inside. Watching the cars pass Jeff Walker could only consider what had been. One of his wait staff refreshed his coffee. As they left, a memory not thought of for years suddenly occurred to him.

"I wonder how Ms. Harris would take to the knowledge of her new boyfriend and his maternal relationship?"

Another sip of bitter coffee. At least it was hot this time. Could he actually share that story with her? Greg and he had been best mates at the time, sworn to secrecy. But that was then, this was now. Now he had something Jeff wanted back. Perhaps this was the only way to get that something good back into his life.

It wasn't long after that experience Ray, Jr. had died leaving Jeff as the only child, the focus of his parents hopes, dreams, as well as their fears. Jeff also found it interesting that at the same time he became an only child, Greg had went from that status to big brother of his little sister Lizbeth.

Something else curious about that as well. At first, he couldn't quite put a finger on it. Suddenly it was all very clear to him. Lizbeth couldn't have been born much more than nine months after Greg had shared his little secret.

"That couldn't be possible. Could it?"

ABOUT THE AUTHOR

James was born in Hollywood, California during the spring of 1965 but quickly found himself relocated to the East Coast. Over the first eighteen years of his life, home was in Pennsylvania, North and South Carolina, Georgia and Florida. For many, this kind of movement could have spelled disaster, but James drew strength of personality while learning to reinvent himself with every change of location. Boldly trekking across the country after high school, James met up with his brother, John in Berkeley and eventually attended U.C. Berkeley.

Today James resides in St. Helena, CA overlooking the amazing Napa Valley. He spent over half a decade exploring various communities in the Verde Valley. He misses his mother, Linda Lee, his sister and her husband, Stacey and Mike, and his niece and nephew-in-law, Candice and Anthony, their son, Antoine and the latest(?) addition, Arianna Love.

www.ingramcontent.com/pod-product-compliance
Lightning Source LLC
Chambersburg PA
CBHW060937120626
46557CB00003B/1031